The Storm

D1364021

Stan Rogow Productions · Grosset & Dunlap

GROSSET & DUNLAP
Published by the Penguin Group
Penguin Group (USA) Inc., 375 Hudson Street, New York, New York 10014, U.S.A.
Penguin Group (Canada), 90 Eglinton Avenue East, Suite 700, Toronto, Ontario, Canada M4P 2Y3
(a division of Pearson Penguin Canada Inc.)
Penguin Books Ltd, 80 Strand, London WC2R 0RL, England
Penguin Ireland, 25 St Stephen's Green, Dublin 2, Ireland
(a division of Penguin Books Ltd)
Penguin Group (Australia), 250 Camberwell Road, Camberwell, Victoria 3124, Australia
(a division of Pearson Australia Group Pty Ltd)
Penguin Books India Pvt Ltd, 11 Community Centre, Panchsheel Park, New Delhi - 110 017, India
Penguin Group (NZ), Cnr Airborne and Rosedale Roads, Albany, Auckland 1310, New Zealand
(a division of Pearson New Zealand Ltd)
Penguin Books (South Africa) (Pty) Ltd, 24 Sturdee Avenue, Rosebank, Johannesburg 2196, South Africa

Penguin Books Ltd, Registered Offices:
80 Strand, London WC2R 0RL, England

Published by Grosset & Dunlap, a division of Penguin Young Readers Group, 345 Hudson Street, New
York, New York 10014. GROSSET & DUNLAP is a trademark of Penguin Group (USA) Inc. Printed in
the U.S.A.

Library of Congress Cataloging-in-Publication Data

Strickland, Brad.
The storm : a novelization / by Brad Strickland.
p. cm. -- (Flight 29 down ; #4)
"Adapted from the teleplays by D.J. MacHale. Based on the TV series created by D.J. MacHale, Stan
Rogow."
ISBN 0-448-44130-6 (pbk.)
I. MacHale, D.J. II. Rogow, Stan. III. Stan Rogow Productions. IV. Title. V. Series.
PZ7.S9166Sso 2006
2005037076

10 9 8 7 6 5 4 3 2 1

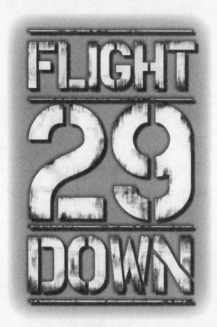

The Storm

**A novelization by
Brad Strickland
Adapted from the
teleplays by D.J. MacHale**

**Based on the
TV series created by
D.J. MacHale
Stan Rogow**

Stan Rogow Productions · Grosset & Dunlap

**For Barbara,
who has been there for
all the adventures**

"What were the lessons imparted by our weeks adrift and our month-long sojourn in the wilderness? We sounded the depths of adversity, and found that adversity can be overcome; we discovered that hunger and thirst can be dealt with if one can hold off despair, more terrible than either; and we learned again the ancient truth that danger, deprivation, and the threat of death can but strengthen the bonds of trust and friendship that any band of adventurers must have, lest they be utterly lost and doomed."

—*Shipwreck and Survival: The Loss of the Schooner Albatross off the Coast of New Guinea, 1888*
Written by Captain Elias Moorcomb, 1894

ONE

Early morning, the day after Abby was found:

Lex

Eight days since our plane crashed. We've been here eight days now. The big kids are getting along okay, I guess. But I keep hoping I can get someone on the radio.

Because eight days is a long time for seven kids—well, eight now, with Abby—to be alone on a deserted island. We don't have any adults around at all. The pilot, Captain Russell, left with three of the kids to search the island for any sign of people. I can't help thinking that's a mistake.

See, I thought people would be looking for us. I expected that sooner or later a search plane would fly over and catch sight of 29 DWN, our crashed plane. Only the search plane hasn't come.

But by now they must be flying search patterns, looking for us. So that means they might come close enough at any time to hear us if I can keep the radio going. If we can pull together that long. Jackson has been doing what he can, and I guess Nathan has been trying hard. Melissa's okay. She does whatever Jackson says needs to be done. And my big sister, Daley, well, she can be bossy, but she's pitched in, too. I just wish that Eric and Taylor would help out more.

Lex switched off the video camera. The sun was barely up, but his skin already felt prickly from past days of sunburn. The tropical glare reflected off the blue ocean, off the small white-capped waves dancing in the blue-green lagoon where their DeHavilland Heron had come roaring in for a crash landing.

The plane itself, cream-white on the top of the fuselage, with a turquoise stripe beneath that, was otherwise all silvery metal except for the blackened starboard wing and the long streaks of soot along that side, showing where two of the engines had caught fire. Everywhere else, the metal reflected the blinding sunlight.

Good. If a rescue plane did chance to fly over, the brilliant reflection would be easier to spot than the two canvas tents, even easier than the billowing white smoke from a signal fire.

Lex turned his head, idly scanning the beach. Eric and Taylor lay on the sand not far from the undamaged wing. Taylor was working on her tan and her highlights.

Eric was just hanging around Taylor. The two of them were always either complaining or, in the case of Eric the practical joker, planning some trick to play on the others.

Melissa was stirring, too. Lex saw her carrying water toward the fire pit. He could hear her voice, rising and falling as she sang a song, though he couldn't catch her words.

He sighed. Sometimes Lex wondered if he were the only one who really understood how serious their situation was.

What good did that do, though? It wasn't as though any of them would actually *listen* to him.

Well—Daley would, sometimes. And if it had to do with electronics, he had showed them that he knew what he was talking about when he got the solar cells out and rigged a way to keep the batteries charged. And he was pretty sure the radio was working okay. Unfortunately, no one was close enough to hear a distress call or for him to hear their radio chatter.

Lex popped the videotape out of the camera. Everyone was keeping a video diary.

It was one small way to keep sane.

Lex replaced the camera in its container so it would be ready for the next person who needed it.

The sun climbed higher, turning the two tents into brilliant white canvas domes against the green backdrop of undergrowth.

People were moving, getting ready for breakfast.

Time to check the radio again.

And the next day:

Everyone slept a little late. They had partied the night before. Abby had organized a dance to try to raise everybody's spirits.

In the girls' tent, Taylor, Melissa, and Daley lay in a kind of triangle, head to foot to head. Taylor was always quick to complain if one of the others had an inch of her space. They spread out as much as possible.

In the boys' tent, spreading out was impossible. The tent was too small to accommodate four bodies, two of them long and lanky, one at least average, and only one short and compact.

So the boys tended to wake up first, when the early rays of the sun began to warm the island, and the inside of the tent, already humid and hot from their body heat, became a sauna.

They also tended to wake up grumbling and groggy from too little sleep.

Eric was first that morning. "Hey, Lex! How can a little guy like you have such big feet?"

"Huh? Wha'? What about my feet?"

Eric gave them a shove with his own foot. "Move 'em!"

Then Jackson: "Ugh! Lex, what was that about?"

"Eric pushed me!"

"He had his feet stuck over in my space!"

With a grunt, Nathan pushed himself up. "Guys!"

"What time is it?" asked Eric with a yawn. "Like four A.M.?"

"It's seven twenty," Lex said.

Jackson wormed his way to a sitting position. "Time to get moving, then."

Eric pointedly rolled over on his side. "Oh, please."

Nathan was pulling on his moss green T-shirt. "Come on, Eric. We know you're not sick."

Eric moaned. "I'm still recuperating. A shellfish allergy can be deadly if you—"

"Get *up.*" Jackson was already dressed in his camo pants and tight-woven black mesh shirt. "If

I put *my* foot into your space, Eric, you'll feel it."

All of them bleary-eyed, all still a little tired, they came out of the boys' tent into the sun. The sea stretched before them, wide and beautifully blue, the incoming waves foaming into snowy surf. It was gorgeous.

And very empty.

The girls' tent flap opened, and Melissa stuck her head out, yawning. "Is Abby already out there?"

"Do you see Abby?" Eric asked.

"Maybe she's gone for water or something," Lex suggested.

"Come on, let's get started," Nathan said in a loud voice. "Another day in Paradise."

Before long, they found the note. Abby had left them again, going north to look for Captain Russell, Jory, and Ian. Melissa couldn't help worrying. Days before, Captain Russell had taken off into the jungle with the three kids. The pilot had *said* they needed to explore the island. But then they had found Abby, who had been separated from the other three. She was dehydrated and unconscious, and they had hauled her back to camp and nursed her back to health.

And some time this morning Abby had slipped away, heading back into the wilderness to find Russell and the other kids.

You had to respect that. Melissa knew that as she had made a choice to stay at camp, Abby had made her choice, too.

Still . . . as Daley oversaw breakfast that morning (fruit and water, none of the emergency MRE food-bar rations that they were trying to save), Melissa kept scanning the dark green line where the jungle began, her eyes anxious.

The jungle, and beyond that the sharp purple slopes of the distant mountains.

Anything could happen out there.

"Here!"

Daley's sharp voice, no doubt repeating what she had already said, snapped Melissa out of her reverie. With one hand, Melissa pushed her hair out of her face. She pulled her canvas hat on, trying to control her two black ponytails whipping in the morning wind, and took the bananas from Daley.

"Thanks," Melissa said with as much of a smile as she could muster.

But her thoughts kept straying. Where was Abby? Would she find the others? Or—

Some things didn't bear thinking about. Melissa began to eat her breakfast.

Lex, the youngest kid on the island, ate as if he had been starved. But it really wasn't that he was hungry. He was just in a hurry to get back to work on the radio.

He had already taken a shift with the radio that morning, sending out another distress call.

In return, he heard only static, the crackling whispers of storms somewhere out at sea, beyond their range of vision. Lightning hundreds of miles away stabbed through angry boiling clouds, and its echo snapped and fried in the radio speakers.

It sounded like an animal. *Scratch. Scratch. Scratch . . .*

Lex thought, *Maybe the antenna's the problem. I've raised it on a ten-foot bamboo pole, but what if that's not high enough? Maybe if we could get it up really high, up in a tree, maybe. Or maybe if we could make a bigger antenna somehow, then it might have the range we need. What would that take? Wire and—what?*

He finished his banana and looked around. Everyone else was eating more slowly. If you eat slowly, Nathan had told them with an air of experience, the food goes farther. He said he had learned that from a book written by his great-great-grandfather, who had been a famous explorer.

Lex took a long drink of lukewarm water. If only a search plane would come.

Anyone flying over the island would have to notice the downed plane.

Wouldn't they?

Nearly eight o'clock. Nathan walked away from the camp to the spot he tended to think of as his private retreat. He carried the video camera and popped his tape in. He carefully set the camera in the fork of a tree, then pressed record and stepped back.

Nathan

Day, uh, nine. Funny, I almost lost track there for a second.

Well, we're still here. Lex thinks search planes are looking for us. God, I hope he's right. He's smarter than I gave him credit for at first. I mean, he has the radio going. Kinda going. If a search plane flies over, I think we could contact it.

Uh, let me see. Oh, yeah, Abby has left us. She took Taylor's backpack and some gear and went to look for Captain Russell and the other two kids. I hope she makes it. I hope they find their way back to camp.

Though if they do, Abby will have to watch out for Taylor. She's pretty mad about the backpack thing.

So to sum up, we're doing okay, I guess. We have food, though it's kind of monotonous. And we have water. Thanks to Daley.

Uh, Daley. She and I got off on the wrong foot at first, I mean competing for the leadership and all. But I have to admit, now that everyone else elected Jackson leader, Daley's a lot easier to take. She's got everything together. She, uh, her organizing—

What am I saying? I might as well admit it, since nobody is ever going to see this except me.

I guess the truth is that I sort of like her. Okay, I guess I have a thing for her, actually.

Of course, I've probably blown my chances with her already. I was sure that I'd make a better leader, and I guess I sort of let her know that. Maybe a little too much and too often. And nothing I've done has quite worked out. Couldn't catch water with a solar still. Couldn't start a fire. Couldn't find food on my own.

Oh, well. Maybe Lex can get someone on the radio. Maybe a rescue plane will come for us.

Or . . . well, maybe not.

Either way, I'd like it if I could—I mean, I'd like to find a way—to be able to find a way to let Daley know how I feel.

Now I'm just babbling.

TWO

Jackson stood on the beach as the others came down in a straggling line. He had rolled up the legs of his camo pants and had waded into the lagoon, ready to cast his baited hook if any morning-feeding fish showed up in the lagoon.

Warm water lapped his bare legs as he concentrated on peering through the surface reflections. The few fish he saw sped past, too small for him. He decided to try for one anyway as a school of some kind of fish about as long as the palm of his hand cruised past his legs. Unfortunately, the second he dropped the hook into the water, they all flashed away.

Man, that was frustrating. After fifteen disappointing minutes, he came slopping up out of the surf and rolled down his pants legs as the rest of the kids crunched onto the sand. He sighed. Why did they all have to give him that *look*? That what-do-we-do-now-boss look?

Hey, he hadn't asked to be their leader. For that matter, he hadn't even run in the election.

But they had voted for a leader, and he was it. So now the other kids gave him the *look*, and whenever something had to be done, they waited for his decision.

Seven kids from LA, and none of them with any survival smarts. No, maybe that was too harsh. Nathan had picked up a lot of ideas from his reading, things he knew about but couldn't manage to do. Daley had at least kept them organized in the first few hours after the crash landing, and Melissa did her share of the work and more. Lex, the youngest, was also the one who really knew things, technical stuff about electricity and radios. Jackson had to smile when he thought back to the party and the way Lex had rigged speakers for the mp3 player so they could dance. Lex was pretty cool.

"Fishing?" Nathan asked with a gesture at the lagoon.

Jackson shrugged but didn't bother replying. Was it fishing if you never even got a bite?

Daley crossed her arms over her bright red sleeveless top. "Well, if the fish aren't available, we really could use more coconuts. They have more calories than the bananas. Want to help me get some?"

Jackson nodded. He had been raised in a city. Before coming to this island, he had never climbed a tree in his life.

But you did what you had to. As hard as it looked, you could learn to climb a coconut tree, as he had already discovered. He shouldered his spear and followed Daley up the sloping beach.

Out of the corner of his eye he saw Lex crouching down over the radio, fiddling with the controls. He heard the faint rasp of static, like something scratching at the speakers with long fingernails.

Scratch ... scratch ... scratch ...

... now slip into the girls' tent. Carefully.

The boys' tent had smelled of sweaty feet. This one holds the floral fragrances of Daley's sunscreen, of Taylor's perfume.

Quickly, though. They're all away at the moment, but who knows when they'll be back? Okay, they have to be here somewhere. Where would people hide them? In their backpacks, of course. Or maybe in this big fabric shopping bag. No. Only makeup, brushes, a comb, and a mirror here.

A noise outside, someone walking through the crackling dry grass!

Duck under the blue sleeping bag, quick! Pull it over and lie absolutely still, freeze. If it's one of the girls coming in—

Footsteps swishing through the coarse grass, and they seem to be passing by.

So raise the corner of the sleeping bag and risk a peek out.

Through the mesh window, a glimpse of somebody walking past the tent, on the way toward the banana trees. Khaki shorts, long legs.

Gone.

Okay, toss off the sleeping bag. Hurry, though. Now try this backpack. Yes, something is rattling in it. Turn the backpack upside down, shake it out onto the green groundcloth of the tent.

Yes! A videotape cartridge!

Hand-lettered label on it:

Melissa.

Grab it. Stuff it into the bag that already holds four videotapes, the ones taken from the boys' tent next door.

Now for the next one ...

Reach for another backpack ...

Melissa really meant to be reasonable. She meant to be calm. She meant to be forceful.

It's simple, she had told herself, fighting down her rage and despair. *Walk up to Taylor—there she is lying on the beach, in her pastel polka-dotted two-piece, catching rays, as usual—and simply tell her in a level, even voice—*

Her pep talk to herself didn't work all that well, because when she opened her mouth, what came out was a tremble of anger as Melissa looked down at the sunbathing Taylor: "Give it back!"

Taylor's eyes flew wide open, and she squinted up as if truly puzzled. "Give *what* back?"

Melissa fought for control. She felt her hands balling up into fists, and she felt a hard lump in her throat. *Stay on top of it. Don't let her goad you. That's just what she wants—to make you cry or to see you beg.*

She swallowed hard. "My video." When Taylor just gave her that empty airheaded stare, she added, "I know you took it!"

Taylor rolled her eyes as she raised up on her elbows. In an annoyed voice, she replied, "Why would I want to watch your boring old video? I'd rather watch my toenails grow!" And sure enough, she glanced down at her feet, as though she'd expected to see some development taking place down there. Taylor pushed her blond hair back, and with an insincere smile and in a falsely friendly voice she chirped, "Speaking of which, do you have any nail polish that I could borrow? Look, the salt water is eating away the—"

Melissa blasted out an impatient breath. "Don't act all innocent! You already watched my video and played it for everybody—remember?"

Taylor shrugged and with an unconcerned half-smile she lowered herself back down to her beach towel. "Oh. Right. Well, there's your proof."

When Melissa didn't move, Taylor sniffed. "I mean, I don't do encores." She made a fluttering, dismissive gesture with her fingers, as if shooing away a pesky fly. "Go bother someone else."

Melissa raised both hands and clenched the air in frustration. "Oh!" She turned on her heel, nearly losing her balance in the hot sand of the beach, and strode away, telling herself that she'd been an idiot, expecting to intimidate Taylor into returning what she had taken.

It didn't help that Taylor yelled after her: "And find me some nail polish!"

Daley was angry and upset. She rummaged through her backpack one last time, just in case.

Nothing.

Clenching her teeth, she pushed aside the flap and ducked out of the girls' tent.

And saw her little brother, Lex. Well, stepbrother. He didn't look happy, but he glanced her way, nailing her with his quizzical eyes.

Daley took three deep, calming breaths, but Lex was pretty sharp. He gave her a closer look. His eyebrows rose. "What's wrong?"

She couldn't keep a growl out of her voice: "Somebody took my video."

Lex stared at her for a moment and then

blurted, "Mine's gone, too! And so is Jackson's."

Daley let the backpack swing at her side. She stood there for a moment, the muggy morning air heavy in her lungs, the early sun already hot on her skin. It felt the way it had the day they had crashed, when a tropical storm was lashing the island. She tilted her head, staring down at Lex. "Are you serious?"

Lex nodded solemnly.

Daley looked around. No one else was in sight. Beyond the trees, the blue ocean rolled in, the breakers white-foamed. White clouds flecked the sky, building up to a low gray mass all along the far horizon.

She shook her head. "Lex, this is bad. Everybody's private thoughts are on those videos. If they get passed around—"

Lex nodded, ducking his head. "Yeah. I know. It'll be war."

He looked back up, his large eyes filled with the same worry and doubt that Daley felt inside.

THREE

The fire pit had become the place for decision making. That's where all seven of them met to divide chores, debate options, and argue points. Oh, and complain. Some of them led the league in complaining.

None of them looked happy that morning. Daley waited for Jackson to say something. They had elected him leader, after all, ignoring her qualifications.

When he didn't, she stated the obvious. "Okay. Everyone's videos are gone. That means one of us is a thief."

She didn't know just what she expected, but what she got were five blank, annoyed looks. And one angry glance from Lex, who turned it like a searchlight on the others. When no one else spoke up, he burst out, "They're private! It's wrong to watch them, or show them to anybody else."

No one spoke, though Nathan nodded encouragement, his big bush of hair stirring in the morning wind. The others just stared back at Lex, except for Taylor, who was frowning critically at her fingernails.

Lex turned away from them and muttered, "It's just . . . wrong!"

To Daley's surprise, Taylor stopped her nail examination and took a step forward. "Hey, it's really not such a big deal. I can understand if somebody wants to, like, watch me." She flashed what she probably thought was a dazzlingly gorgeous smile at Jackson and Nathan. With a giggle, she said, "Come on, I don't really care. But after you're done, give it back, okay?" She half-turned to include Eric in on the glory of her smile. "'Cause I need that video."

Nathan grunted and leaned toward Melissa. Daley heard him say, "Taylor thinks her tape's gonna make her a TV star!"

Taylor's simper became an angry glare. She snapped, "I do not!" Then, with a smug smile tossed to Eric—Daley thought he looked like a dog being thrown a puppy treat—"It's gonna make me a *movie* star!"

For a couple of seconds, Eric just stood looking back at Taylor with a goofy grin on his face. Then he snapped his fingers and pushed his straw hat back on his head. "Hey! I know what must've happened to our videos! I'll bet you Abby took 'em when she left!"

Daley shook her head. Eric could be funny sometimes, but he could also be a major pain. "No way," she told him flatly. "Look, think about it. Abby went into the jungle searching for Captain Russell, Ian, and Jory. Why on earth would she want to take videotapes?"

Eric shrugged, scratching his chest idly. "How should I know? Maybe she could braid 'em together and make a rope. Or, hey, she could make a little tiny fort with the cassettes and pretend—"

Nathan raised his voice and overrode Eric's speculations: "Daley's right. Abby didn't take them. She couldn't have. I made a recording *after* she left, so it definitely wasn't her."

As though determined to make some kind of point—any kind of point—Eric said, "Well, maybe she sneaked back into camp and . . ." He seemed to realize that no one was paying attention to him, and his voice trailed off.

Daley raised both of her hands for attention. When everyone was looking at her, she said, as calmly as she could, "Look, right now it's no harm, no foul." Jackson's face was, as usual, impassive. Nathan, who had been Daley's chief rival for leadership—at least she had *thought* he was before the others unanimously voted for Jackson—gave her an encouraging nod. Quietly, reasonably, Daley went on, "We all agree it was wrong to take them, right? So—"

Taylor giggled again. "Hey, not *all* of us agree!" When six suspicious glances darted her way, she sounded defensive: "I mean, someone must *not* agree, right? Because obviously, *somebody* took them."

Nathan seemed to understand that Daley had just about reached her limit with Taylor's and Eric's careless take on the situation. He said slowly, "Right." Then he took a step forward and addressed the entire group: "Look, whoever it was, you can understand how seriously we're taking this. This is like—like reading someone's private mail, or breaking into someone's room. I agree with Daley. If the videos are returned, we'll forget about the whole thing, okay? So let's say that if the tapes are returned to their owners by this afternoon, this just goes away. We'll forget it ever happened. No investigation, no punishment, nothing. Okay?"

Daley said, "Right." Then, after an odd moment of hesitation, people began to nod and murmur agreement. She couldn't help glancing at each of them as her suspicions bubbled.

Eric? He was the joker in the pack, but so far he'd been more of an annoyance than, well, a thief. He *looked* serious enough at the moment, but still—and then there was Taylor.

Taylor just didn't get it. She still thought of

their crash landing as just a little vacation. Her mantra was "We won't be here long, right?" And she was capable of thoughtlessness, like the time she had left the video camera running and had exhausted the batteries. Still, it was a long step from being an airhead to stealing.

Nathan? Well, he had been her bitter rival back at school, when they had run against each other for the presidency of the class. And he was full of tales about how his great-grandfather or something had been this intrepid explorer— really kind of boring, and no matter how good his ancestor had been, Nathan frankly just didn't cut it as a leader. Somehow, though, she didn't see him as a sneak.

Melissa . . . no way, Daley decided. She's too quiet, too shy. Melissa went along with the crowd, she didn't make waves—but then, didn't they always say you had to watch out for the quiet ones?

Jackson. The outsider. A great big question mark, really. A recent transfer to the school. No one knew him very well. Jackson hardly ever talked, and he did things his own way.

Lex? He was a serious kid who read everything. He was a lot older than his ten birthdays would lead you to think. Then, too, Daley remembered how upset he had been when she had brought up the subject of the missing videos.

Eric jolted Daley out of her reverie. "Hey,

what's wrong with you? You've seen us before, remember?"

Daley blinked. She shook her head and then said, "Look, whoever took 'em, don't be an idiot. And don't watch them. Just—just give them back."

They all seemed to agree, nodding and murmuring. But as they turned away, as they headed for the jobs they had all agreed to do, Daley stared after them. She caught more than one of them darting a suspicious look back her way.

They couldn't think that *she* had anything to do with the theft.

Could they?

Coconuts didn't grow the way Nathan had always pictured them, certainly not the way they grew in animated cartoons. They didn't hang in clusters like big brown hairy grapes at the top of palm trees.

No, they came wrapped in fibrous, lumpy brownish-gray husks. To get at the nut inside, you first had to peel the husk away. Then, of course, you *still* had the nut to deal with.

Hairy and dark brown and—hard to crack.

Nathan and Melissa were working together on a pile of coconuts. Jackson had sharpened a stake and had planted it in the ground. With a cooler as a brace, it worked okay. You forced the husk against the point until it penetrated. Then you peeled the husk away from the nut.

Not exactly the career Nathan would have chosen for himself, coconut husker. It made his shoulders ache and raised blisters on the palms of his hands when he had been pounding away for a while. But he worked at the task, getting the husks broken open so that Melissa could peel the fibers away.

He couldn't help noticing how distressed Melissa looked. "Come on," he said as he reached for another nut. "It's okay."

Melissa's voice betrayed how upset she was: "It's not like I have anything to hide," she said darkly. "At least not since Taylor broadcast my tape saying how I liked Jackson."

Her tone had lapsed into such a little-sister complaint that Nathan couldn't hold back a chuckle. "Yeah, that was pretty funny." He gulped as Melissa's dark eyes flashed at him, a look of pure anger. "I meant *lousy*," he said, hastily trying to backtrack. "Uh, did I say *funny*? I meant *lousy*."

For a moment he couldn't tell if Melissa was about to burst into tears or join him in a rueful laugh. She did neither. Instead, she dropped her gaze to the coconut she was working on and muttered, "It's all right. I'm over that. Right now

I'm more upset that one of us is a thief. It's so wrong."

Nathan paused to toss his head, clearing his windblown hair from his face. "Yeah, well," he said. He glanced around. No one was close enough to hear them over the background crash and grumble of the incoming surf. He lowered his voice to a conspiratorial murmur: "I'd just as soon not have anyone see *my* tape."

Melissa lifted her eyebrows in what looked like shock.

"Not that I said anything bad about anyone! Because I didn't—I'm not the kind to gossip, anyway," he hastily added. His face felt unusually hot, and his voice became sheepish as he reluctantly confessed, "But—well, I sort of, kind of admitted that I have a thing for . . . uh, Daley."

Melissa's eyes widened. "You *what*?"

Oh, great, *now* she looked as if she were about to start laughing. Nathan scowled. "*Shh!* I'm telling you, not the world."

With a dubious shake of her head, Melissa replied, "You *like* Daley? But you two are always fighting."

"Tell me about it," Nathan agreed. He tossed a coconut to her and picked up another one. "That one's ready."

Melissa started to rip the tough fibers of the husk away from the nut. In a voice that was a bit too casual, she asked, "So what made you realize you, uh, had this thing for Daley?"

Nathan's cheeks felt like they were about to catch fire. He hacked at the coconut, trying to pound it squarely on the sharpened stake. You had to be careful not to impale your hand, or—

"Answer me," Melissa said.

Nathan attempted an unconcerned shrug. "Uh, well, you know. She does have a knack for organizing us."

Melissa actually did give a little snort of laughter at that. "Oh, wonderful. That's every girl's secret dream, you know. For some guy to tell her, 'Hey, you're a great . . . organizer.' "

With a defeated grin, Nathan admitted, "I know, I know. But she actually is pretty cool. Not that I'd tell her that. She'd laugh me right off the planet." Another whack, and the stake finally broke through the covering over the coconut. Nathan made a mental note: He'd have to get Jackson to sharpen the stake again. He dropped the nut and said to Melissa, "Don't you tell anybody, either. Okay?"

Melissa gave him a reproachful look. "You know I wouldn't!"

"Thanks."

Melissa's face took on a devilish smile. "Because if that ever got out, you'd really be slaughtered! You and Daley—that's really pretty funny!"

Nathan scowled at her in surprise.

Mischievously, Melissa said, "Oh, did I say *funny*? I meant *lousy*!"

Nathan rolled his eyes and supposed that he'd asked for that one.

FOUR

Taylor was beginning to regret ever coming on this stupid trip. It was supposed to have been so great and all, an eco-camping adventure on the tropical island of Palau, wherever that was. The brochures had been, like, all blue water and sandy white beaches and colorful kayaks and underwater photos of fish.

Well, so far none of that had come true. Except for the beach. The beach was okay, but it would have been nicer with a few waiters to bring her sodas when she wanted.

She should have been suspicious about the whole thing from the very beginning, when they'd asked her to work at making the trip happen. It was this school spirit thing. Everyone had to pitch in and help out. They'd had car washes and bake sales and all sorts of fund-raisers.

But no one could accuse her of slacking. Taylor had done her bit. She'd posed for posters advertising every single stupid thing the others had done to raise the money.

It wasn't fair, now, being stuck on this dumb island along with these—these losers.

She would rise above it, though. This was the kind of adventure that could get you on TV talk shows. And TV talk shows could be a stepping-stone to the big screen. Maybe she could even star in a movie based on her heroic struggle to lead the others in a fight for survival.

If only—

"Hey," Eric said, hurrying up to fall in step beside her, breaking her train of thought.

She walked along the high-water mark, the wind from the lagoon gusting in, tossing her blond hair. Swimming was fun, but the salt was bad for her hair, and the others were so unreasonable about her very real need to wash and condition her hair, and what if she started to run low on shampoo—

"So, bad luck losing your audition tape," Eric said. He had been her cameraman. Even goofs like Eric had their uses.

But what he said reminded Taylor that she was angry. Furious, in fact. "I didn't *lose* it, some loser *stole* it! I hope whoever took it has the decency to give it back after he enjoys my performance," she snapped.

"You could always make another tape, you know," Eric suggested. "In fact, when we get back to civilization, I'd be only too glad to talk to my dad about getting you a break in show business."

Oh, yeah, that was right. Eric's dad was a comedian. He'd even been on a few TV shows or something. Taylor turned to Eric, making her face a mask of tragic suffering. "Thanks, but I'm not worried about that right now. This is serious!"

"Well, sure—"

Her anger broke through again. She jabbed a finger at Eric. "Listen, nobody can leave this island until I get my tape back!"

He blinked at her, and then—he laughed! He actually laughed at her! "Good call," he said with that big, wide doofus grin of his. "Okay, we'll make sure nobody leaves until you get your tape . . ."

She nodded.

". . . and until we find a boat," Eric added. "There is that little detail, you know."

Taylor shook her head. She would never understand how boys' minds worked. If you could even call what buzzed around inside their heads minds. "Aren't you upset?" she demanded.

Eric tilted his straw hat to one side, like he thought it made him look rakish. That was a word she had picked up in a teen magazine, describing a male actor who was in what the mag called the Junior Brat Pack.

Taylor didn't exactly know what it meant, but

she remembered the word and how smug the actor in the photos had looked—and if looking smug was rakish, then Eric was definitely rakish. Then, as if he had been considering her question, Eric gave an irritating leer. "Upset, me? Nah. Some people on this island may have something deep and dark in their past to hide. I don't."

She gave him a suspicious, narrow-eyed appraisal and asked, "What does that mean?" Eric winked at her. "Come on," she insisted. "What do you know?" Then she dropped her voice: "Did you take the tapes?"

A gust of wind threatened to snatch Eric's hat, but he made a grab for it and pinned it down. "Maybe," he said coyly.

"What does that mean?"

"And maybe not," he added. "But I can pretty much guarantee that when things start coming out in the open—when we find out what's actually down on tape—well, we're gonna have ourselves a whole lot of fireworks." He laughed and turned away. "See ya."

Taylor watched him saunter off toward the camp, one hand still clamped on his stupid hat. What was he up to? How could she find out?

And . . . what did he mean with that remark about fireworks? What would happen when they discovered who had actually taken the tapes?

A gust of wind off the lagoon suddenly whipped sand against her bare legs, driving the thought out of her mind. "Ouch!" In the whipping wind, she did a little irritated dance and wondered how long it would be before someone found them and took them off this stupid island.

Daley supposed that she worried too much. She always had, ever since the bad years when her mother had been so ill and her dad, the famous filmmaker, spent all his time with her in the hospital.

Somehow, Daley had held things together then. No one at school had even suspected the turmoil she was going through. And after her mother passed away and her dad remarried, she'd thought it was time for her to relax, finally.

Except she couldn't. Taking control, doing things her way, had become too much of a habit for her to become, well, carefree. She just wasn't built that way. As the breezes from the ocean buffeted the plane, she worked on, the responsible one, the careful one, the one who—face it—had to nag the others into taking care of business.

Well, things weren't too bad at the moment. Right now they had enough food—though the shellfish had caused Eric to have a bad allergic reaction, and people were pretty sure to get tired of bananas and coconuts soon. Most of the snacks they had brought on board had been eaten, but some of the supplies meant for their camping trip were left, and although they had punctured the life raft, they still had a bag of MRE food-bar emergency rations, enough for maybe three days if they were careful.

And even when all the rest of the food was gone, well, there *were* plenty of bananas. What was that stupid old joke? "My people, I have bad news and good news. The bad news is that all we have to eat are buffalo chips. The good news is— we've got plenty of buffalo chips!"

Bananas, morning, noon, and night. The banana diet. The hot new path to weight loss and buffness. You, too, can have the body of a chimp.

It was the kind of joke she never made aloud. Daley counted and then transferred some pouches of dried food from a bag to a plastic bin. Safer there, easier to keep an eye on—hmm. The video camera was in the bin, too. That's where Lex had advised them to keep it, to make sure it stayed dry and protected from the salt air.

Well, the camera wouldn't hurt anything. Daley packed the last of the food around it and started to replace the lid.

Then she hesitated and reached for the video camera. It was a good one, compact and light, with its own liquid-crystal screen and even a small speaker for sound playback. Lucky that Lex had found a way to use solar cells to recharge the battery.

Of course, without tapes, it wasn't much good.

Daley turned the camera, staring down into the lens.

Hmm . . .

She replaced the camera and snapped the lid back on the plastic bin. That one was full. She carefully stowed it in the shelter of the plane, then picked up an empty bin. It would be handy for the fruit the others would be bringing in—should have already brought in by now, in fact.

She walked up the slope toward their campsite. Nathan was there already, sitting on one of the orange-and-black airplane seats they had ripped out of the fuselage. He had dropped a sack of husked coconuts beside him, and he was leaning forward with a look of concentration.

Daley walked up behind him, then stood for a moment, holding her plastic bin and watching him. "What are you doing—making sure nobody steals the tents next?"

Nathan gave a little start of surprise and looked back at her. "No. I'm trying to figure out who took the tapes. You know, logically."

"By staring at the tents?" She glanced at them. The boys' tent on the left, canvas and dark gray. The girls' tent on the right, canvas and red. A cooler, a plastic water container, another green plastic bin just like the one she carried. Scene of the crime. "What are you, psychic or something?"

Nathan laughed and turned back around.

Leaning forward, he said, "No, it's a little more scientific than that. The tapes were in our packs, and the packs were in the tents. I'm trying to think back to when somebody was here alone and had the chance to grab 'em. See, a crime occurs when someone has a motive for doing it, the means to do it—and in this case, the opportunity. That's the key. Figuring out who had the opportunity."

Daley raised her eyebrows, fighting the urge to grin at how enthusiastic his voice had become. Nathan sounded like a little kid sometimes. Well, maybe a *serious* little kid, like Lex. "Oh. Cool." She set the bin down and came to stand behind Nathan. "Okay, can I play?"

"Um—sure," Nathan said, sounding surprised at her request.

Daley's heart was beating a little too fast. Something was tickling the back of her mind, something about the videos or . . . something. She casually leaned one arm on the back of the airplane seat and tried to make her voice sound offhand, unconcerned. "Wait, though. First tell me—did you take them?"

Nathan spun on her, his face registering his surprise and shock. "No!" he protested at once, sounding appalled at the very idea. But before Daley could relax, he hit her with a question in return: "Did *you*?"

Her first reaction was a hot flare of anger. But she bit back a sarcastic response—after all, she had asked first. Daley spread her hands out and gave Nathan an irritated look. "Do you seriously think so?" she asked in as flat and unemotional a tone as she could muster.

Nathan's dark eyes flicked away from her face. "Well, no," he said slowly, though to Daley he sounded somewhat less than a hundred percent sure of that. "I—I guess not."

But she could accept his word. At least for the time being. "Good," she said. "Then I guess we're both innocent."

Nathan nodded in a relieved way.

And then Daley jabbed him again by adding, "Unless proven guilty."

His dark gaze flashed back at her. Was Nathan angry? He looked angry, she thought, angry and upset at the mere suggestion that he might be the thief they were looking for.

Or maybe not angry.

Maybe . . . guilty?

But Nathan swallowed whatever he was feeling and said, "If you want to join in, that's fine with me, but let's move on. Look, when was the last time you remember seeing your tape?"

Daley thought back. She had made an entry on her video diary . . . by firelight. "Last night," she said. "After Abby's dance, just before we turned in. The others were in the tent, and I made the recording by the fire pit. And when I finished, I popped the tape out and put it in the side pocket of my backpack, the same as always."

Nathan nodded. "Last night. Okay, I made a recording this morning, sometime right around eight. That means they weren't stolen during the night."

Despite herself, Daley felt impressed. Nathan was actually going about this in an organized way—something she hadn't particularly noticed about him before. She moved to the airplane seat next to Nathan and carefully lowered herself into it. They had a tendency to shift and dump you out sprawling on the ground if you weren't careful. Thoughtfully, she said, "I remember that Melissa said she realized her tape was missing at about ten o'clock this morning. Maybe not exactly, but that's pretty close to the time."

Nathan nodded. "Good. So let's say the window for the crime was between eight and ten o'clock." He stared back at the tent. When he was concentrating like that, he was really sort of cute.

Daley sighed. What would a boy think if a girl told him, "Hey, you're really organized. I like that."

She'd sound like an idiot.

Besides, this was serious. The seven of them had to stick together. If one was a thief, if one had turned against the others—well, it wasn't a game, it was survival. And survival was as serious as you could get.

Still—

Watching Nathan's grave look of concentration as he stared toward camp, Daley admitted, "You know, if I wasn't so ticked, this would actually be kind of fun."

Nathan nodded as if he had only half heard her. In a thoughtful voice, he murmured, "Really."

The wind plucked at Eric's blue shirt, and he had to hang onto his straw hat to keep it from skimming off on a trajectory toward Micronesia or someplace. He felt vaguely irritated, vaguely satisfied. Taylor could be so touchy, and her sense of humor was approximately the same as an average oyster's.

But—he couldn't help grinning as he thought about how he had left her down the beach—he had intrigued her. He hadn't answered all of her questions, and she was wondering about what he knew and how he knew it. And his dad had always told him that the key was keeping your audience hanging.

Get 'em on the edge of their seats, set 'em up with a good solid build—and then hit them with the payoff.

The fitful wind coming off the ocean should have been fresh and cooling, but it felt heavy, weighted down with humidity. Above him the sun was climbing high, and his stomach was beginning to growl. The tide was low at the moment—funny how that little kid Lex had been the only one of them to think about the tide back on the first day.

Man, it had been so hard, hitched up like a horse or something, leaning against the deadweight, hauling the plane up on the beach as the incoming water lifted it, threatened to wash it out to sea.

Well—that kind of activity was what Jackson's muscles were for. From now on, let him do it. Other people could think and plan, and that was the role Eric saw for himself, really. Not a beast of burden, definitely not.

Eric approached the plane and walked around behind the tail. Even after more than a week had passed, he could still smell the sharp, scorched scent from the two burned-out engines on the right wing.

Eric paused on what Lex insisted on calling the port side of the plane. Meaning the left side, of course. Because if it isn't the right side, it's the one that's *left*—right? Ah, thank you, ladies and gentlemen, I'll be playing this island until— whenever. Remember to tip your waitresses.

Waitresses. Man, right now I'm hungry.

But Daley had imposed rationing. She'd figured out how much they needed, or so she said, and that's what they'd all agreed to eat, not a crumb more. Of course, Daley was no real problem in herself, but that big—and strong—jerk Jackson was backing her up.

However, at the moment, friends, no one seems to be around.

If Eric wasn't mistaken, and he was never mistaken about much of anything, being a very savvy kind of guy, thank you, the pouches of food were in that green plastic bin. That one right there, see, resting on the green tarp. And no one was guarding that green plastic bin, on that little old green tarp, so—

Eric popped the top. O-ho! And aha! Someone, doubtless the very efficient Daley, had actually anticipated his arrival and had stowed away in the bin, ladies and gentlemen, this nice assortment of very yellow, very delectable, ripe and lovely bananas.

How handy. Because whereas a missing pouch of emergency rations just *might* be noticed, a missing banana was simply one of the bunch, right?

And banana peels did not, no sir, have the undesirable property of becoming inconveniently wind-borne after you had eaten the fruit. No suspicious wrapper to explain away, just a limp old banana peel you could slip into the lagoon. Maybe the fish would even like it.

Maybe some of the shellfish that had darn near killed him would feast on a banana peel, and if there was any justice, maybe they would get deathly ill on it.

Grinning, Eric took the banana and closed the lid of the bin.

He barely registered the tarp moving under his feet, but suddenly the world spun in a flash of yellow and blue, and—crash!—he landed on his stomach and chin with an impact that knocked the wind right out of him. Gasping, Eric breathed in a lungful of air and about a teaspoon of flying sand. He felt it gritting in his teeth. Yuck!

"Whoa!" With an effort, he rolled over, still clutching his prize. Eric spat sand, fought for breath, and found himself staring up at Jackson, who looked about a mile and a half tall from down here, a threatening, looming figure silhouetted against blue sky and billowing white cloud.

He was still holding the tarp. Jackson, the rat, had grabbed it and had jerked it out from under Eric's feet. Oh, the bins were okay, they were still right in place, just like the dishes standing neatly on a bare table after a magician yanks away the tablecloth, but Eric—well, he might have serious internal contusions and abrasions. "I think you hurt my spleen," he complained. "I got a sprained spleen here, you spleen sprainer!"

Jackson wasn't laughing. "You're a thief."

Eric groaned. The trouble was that he was marooned on this stupid island with people who didn't appreciate a good punch line. "Oh, give me a break," he muttered. He held up the fruit, slightly squashed because he had involuntarily tightened his grip on it as he did his belly flop into the sand. "You could have broken my ribs with that little trick. And for what? It's a banana!"

Jackson tilted his head, his expression unforgiving.

Eric waggled the fruit. "A banana? Hey, can I appeal to your human side? A banana appeal?"

He might as well have tried to get a laugh out of a coconut tree. "Where are the tapes?" asked Jackson.

Eric blinked up at him, his mouth opening and closing. *Ladies and gentlemen, my crowd-pleasing impression of a beached flounder, ah, thank you very much*—but at last he scowled back up at Jackson, his face indignant. "What! You think I took them?"

Jackson, by far the tallest of all the kids on the island, took a menacing step forward, and Eric froze. He knew better than to push his luck, especially with someone who looked as disgruntled and as menacing as Jackson did at this particular moment. "Where are they?" Jackson asked.

Eric realized that if he could just make it to his feet, he could run in about six possible directions. And he still held on to the banana.

When Jackson didn't immediately pin him down, Eric decided to kid him a little. He gave Jackson a great big grin. From the feel of his teeth, a great big sandy grin. "What's the matter, chief?"

he asked. "Hey, are you worried about something on that tape of yours getting out?"

Faster than Eric had thought possible, Jackson swooped forward, and all of a sudden his finger was prodding Eric in the chest, hard, man, as hard as a stick. Eric sucked in his breath.

What had his dad always told him? "When you think you're flopping, that's no time to back down. Just stick a grin on your face and make with the jokes."

Except this was no joke. Jackson's face was grim, as hard and solemn as a tombstone, and about as expressive. Spacing his words out, he growled, "Bring . . . the . . . tapes . . . back—now!"

When Jackson straightened up again, Eric took the opportunity to scuttle away, *Ah, yes, ladies and gentlemen, my famous impression of a crab in a hurry,* until he was at last beyond range of those intimidating fists, and then he immediately sprang to his feet.

"Whoa," he said in a rueful voice, rubbing the spot on his chest where Jackson had prodded him. "Hey, whatever it is, it must be . . . real *bad* to get you all bent like this."

Jackson didn't move. His glower grew more intense, but at least he didn't take a swing at Eric. At the moment, that put Eric ahead in the game.

"See you around," said Eric. He raised the banana like a cigar, like a prop, and waggled it. "Say good night, Jackson."

Jackson said nothing. For a second he looked as if he were about to explode, but then he mastered his anger. He didn't laugh or even smile. He just turned around and stormed off, up the hill.

Eric spat out some lingering grains of sand and started to peel his hard-won banana.

Jackson. Man, what a jerk he was.

Eric couldn't stand a guy who didn't appreciate a good joke.

FIVE

Melissa's mind kept going back to what Nathan had said.

A thing for Daley.

Daley, of all people! How weird was that?

"Stupid," she muttered, carefully adding wood to the fire. That was one of her jobs—the fire had to be kept going, at least at a low level, even when they weren't cooking. Because, as Lex had pointed out, if a plane should fly over or if a ship should show up on the distant horizon, they could throw some palm fronds and some green wood on even a low fire and instantly have a super-duper smoke signal billowing up, saying "Look at me."

And speaking of Lex, here he came, nearly staggering under the weight of an armload of wood. It was plentiful enough around the edge of the jungle—lots of fallen branches, some of them even dry enough to burn. Lex dropped the wood with a clatter and started to brush the chips and leaves off the front of his shirt.

Melissa couldn't help feeling sorry for Lex. He was so—so *serious* all the time. Well, Daley was serious, but Daley would laugh now and then. In fact, of them all, Lex was the only one she had never seen laugh.

Well, not quite. Jackson. But Jackson was— *mysterious.* That was kind of attractive in a guy.

Lex hung around, his face glum.

Melissa dropped more wood onto the fire, sending up a little cloud of sparks. She watched to make sure they didn't land on anything dry and asked, "Hey, did the tapes show up?"

Morosely, Lex shook his head. A gust of wind ruffled his thick dark hair. He'd be a cute guy—in about six years. "No," he said.

Melissa sighed.

"It's bothering you," Lex said.

Yes. A lot of things bothered Melissa. She said, "I know it's wrong, but I'm kind of curious to know what the others said about me. I guess I can understand why someone might have wanted to take a look at the tapes. Curiosity, you know."

"What if you don't like what the others said?" Lex asked.

"Yeah." Melissa shrugged. "I guess that's possible."

Possible. Likely, even. How many teachers over

the years had told Melissa, "All you need is a little more self-confidence," as if that were something you could go online and order with your mom's credit card.

Lex hunkered down beside the fire. "If the tapes can't be private, I think it's better they're gone for good."

"People could get their feelings hurt," Melissa agreed. "I know." She leaned forward, hugging her legs, resting her chin on her knees. "Still. I'd like to know what they said about me."

She became aware that Lex was staring at her. "Not that I took them," she said hastily.

"Uh—okay."

She jumped up. "Well, I've got a million things to do. You watch the fire for a while, okay? Just be sure this wind doesn't spread it."

"Yeah."

But as she walked away, Melissa could feel Lex's steady gaze. Wondering. Considering.

Accusing.

Nathan couldn't get over how well he and Daley were getting along. This—well, call it this detective work. No, this detective *game*. Anyway, it was fun, sitting here and working through the list of suspects. "Okay," he said. "So we've established that you and I have alibis. We were never alone during the crucial period; we were always with at least one other person."

Daley nodded in agreement and said, "Right. We've been over that. So, who was alone during that time?"

Nathan stared back at the two tents, their sides rippling in the rising wind. "That's the question. Okay, anyone who we can't establish as being somewhere else could have been here."

He caught a teasing glint in Daley's eye. She didn't actually come out and say "Well, *duh*," but her expression implied that.

"Look, I know this is repetitive," Nathan said defensively. "But it's all we have to work with, so bear with me. I made my tape around eight this morning. And at that time, you and Taylor were here."

"She was trying to find some nail polish," Daley said.

"Nail polish."

"The ocean's been very bad for my nails," Daley said with a wickedly accurate approximation of Taylor in midwhine. "Doesn't anybody have at least one bottle?"

Nathan chuckled. "Unbelievable. And right after I popped out my tape and put the camera back in the bin, we all went down to the beach, right?"

"Jackson was already there, remember?"

A memory of Jackson emerging from the

lagoon, his makeshift fishing rod in hand, floated through Nathan's mind. "Right, we met him on the way."

Daley put her chin on her hand. "And then he and I went to collect coconuts. That took us about half an hour or a little longer. Now, where were Lex, Eric, and Melissa?"

Nathan leaned back, his hands crossed behind his head. Why couldn't Daley always be this interested in what he had to say? "Well . . . I saw Lex at the plane, trying to raise someone on the radio. He does that—"

"Four times a day," Daley finished. "I know."

"Let me see . . . when he finished with the radio, he took off with Taylor."

"Jackson went back to the beach after we got the coconuts," Daley said. "I brought the sack of coconuts back here at, what, about nine?"

"It would have been about nine," Nathan agreed. "Right."

"And when I dropped them off, let me see, Lex, Eric, Taylor, and Melissa were all here, too. Taylor was complaining about not having enough water to wash her hair. So then Eric left to go to the well. He asked Lex to go with him to help carry the water."

"*Help* carry it."

Daley sighed at Nathan's sarcastic tone. "I know, I know. You'd think Lex would be too smart to fall for that 'I've been so sick' routine."

"Okay, I'd been down in the plane, and Jackson came and told me the coconuts needed to be husked, so I walked back in to camp, and I remember passing Eric and Lex on the way."

"And you were in the plane—"

"Looking for sunscreen," Nathan said. "I don't burn all that easily, but with this glaring sun—"

"Right," Daley said. "Wait a minute, though. Lex had borrowed my sunscreen."

"Yes, so you ran off to catch him and make sure that he'd put some on."

Daley nodded. "Melissa went with me. I caught up to them, and Lex said he'd left my sunscreen in the boys' tent, so I sent him back to dig it out and put some on. I told him to let you have some, too. Eric talked Melissa into going with him to help lug some water back."

"Yeah, Lex came back and brought the sunscreen to me. I couldn't do much with the coconuts until Melissa got back to help, so I asked everybody if they wanted to go down to the beach and play coconut catch. That seemed to psych Lex up. He said he'd round up everyone— no, wait. He didn't go far, because about then Eric and Melissa came in with the water."

Nathan closed his eyes. *If only I wasn't so brain-dead*, he thought. Lack of sleep had a nasty way of catching up with you. He remembered a time when he'd pulled an all-nighter, staying up until dawn to study for an important history test.

Except he'd blown the test because his brain seemed to have turned to putty. He'd dozed off somewhere between the Battle of Lexington and the Declaration of Independence, and his grade had been—well, not enough to justify a night of studying.

Slowly, he said, "Let me see . . . Taylor thought catch was a stupid game, and she didn't want to play. Big surprise. And she was all upset about something. She went off—looking for you, right?"

"She found me," Daley said. "And you're right, her world was crashing down on her. A button had come off her shirt and she didn't know how to sew it back on."

"You're kidding!" Nathan shook his head.

"She doesn't understand the principle of the needle," Daley explained. "Another big surprise. Helpless."

"Even I can sew a button on," Nathan said.

"*Lex* can sew a button on," Daley returned. "So could Taylor if she wasn't as—what is it?"

"Wait a minute," Nathan said, getting slowly to his feet. "Let me think. Taylor came to you to get her button sewed back on?"

"Yeah," Daley said. "She had the needle and thread and all, but—"

"No, wait. Was anyone else with you?"

"Just Melissa. Why?"

Nathan bit his lower lip. Daley stared at him

with a quizzical expression. He noticed how her hair gleamed in the sun. It was lighter than it had been—the sun bleaching it to a coppery hue. He blinked and said, "Just Melissa. That's it?"

Daley gave a very decided nod. "Yup. What do you reckon it means, Marshal?"

A joke. Daley had made a little joke.

Only Nathan didn't feel like laughing. He said slowly, "Well—Jackson, Eric, and I walked down to the beach and started to toss a coconut around. Lex wasn't with us. He said he was going to find you."

Daley's face froze. Softly, she said, "But he didn't."

The stunned look on her face gave Nathan a pang. He hadn't meant this, not when he'd started the game. Daley looked as if she were about to—cry? Yell? He couldn't be sure.

"No," he said. "Not Lex. That's impossible."

"Totally impossible," Daley agreed.

Together, they both turned and looked back at the tents.

Nathan didn't know what Daley saw there.

What he saw—in his mind's eye, anyway—was Lex. All alone.

S I X

L ex frowned in frustration. No matter what frequency he tried, the radio produced only the scratchy, crackling sound of static.

He tuned the radio to 121500 kilohertz. That was the distress frequency. "Hello, anyone listening. Mayday, Mayday. DeHavilland Heron 29 DWN, flight to Palau, is down. Repeat, DeHavilland Heron Twenty-niner Delta William November is down on an island, location unknown. This is one of the passengers. If anyone hears me, everyone survived the crash. We need to be rescued. If anyone hears me—"

Nothing. Just the raspy scratch of static. Lex sighed and methodically began to check all the other frequencies again, straining to hear anything, the merest whisper of a human voice. Something.

He saw movement from the corner of his eye and glanced up. Daley and Nathan were walking toward him, looking strangely awkward.

Lex grunted in frustration. They'd be hoping he had good news for them. As they came near, he shook his head. "Still nothing but static."

Daley stopped a few feet away and crossed her arms. She glanced at Nathan, who was staring at Lex. When Nathan didn't say anything, Daley cleared her throat. "Um, Lex, you know that I trust you more than anybody."

Lex felt his heart sink. He had been right. Everyone was hoping he could use the radio to call for help. He hung his head and mumbled, "Sorry." Then he took a deep breath. "I've been thinking, maybe we could get the radio antenna up higher. There are some tall palm trees up on the hills, and Jackson's pretty good at climbing—"

Nathan looked unusually serious. "No, it's not that."

Daley seemed to be groping for the right words. With a concerned expression, she said, "Look, I know there's always a good reason for whatever you do."

Now Lex was confused. His big sister was always direct with him, never beating around the bush, even when she was annoyed with him. Lex switched off the crackling radio and asked, "What's the matter, Day?"

Daley just stood there, looking uncomfortable.

Finally, Nathan spoke up: "We figured out that the videotapes were stolen between eight and ten this morning."

Frowning, Lex asked, "So?"

"So you were the only one who was in the campsite alone during that time."

Light dawned. Lex slowly stood up. His voice shook with nervousness: "Wait. You think I took them?"

Neither Daley nor Nathan said anything, but Lex could read the suspicion in their faces. He protested, "Why would I do that?"

And then from behind the plane Eric walked up, a smirk on his face. "Very, very good question!"

Daley's expression became angry. "Eric! Were you eavesdropping?"

"Not cool," Nathan said.

Eric didn't look concerned. He stabbed a finger in Lex's direction. "I always thought it was him. The little thief!"

The wind whipped up again, and Lex squinted against it. He looked uneasily out to the horizon, where the band of dark clouds seemed to be closer, taller. If another storm was building out there—

"Huh?" Daley was speaking, but to Eric, not to him.

Sternly, she said, "But it wasn't him, Eric!"

"He looks pretty guilty to me," Eric returned, that smirk never leaving his face.

Daley turned to him. "You didn't do it. Did you, Lex?"

Frustration welled up in Lex. Couldn't anyone else see the trouble they were in? Couldn't they understand how little chance they had unless they could somehow summon help? Why did they have to get hung up on something as stupid, as—as *trivial* as the video diaries? Clenching his hands, he said, "I don't believe this!" He started to walk away, then broke into a run. He hadn't cried in a long time, but now he felt—

From behind him, Daley yelled, "Lex!"

And overriding her, Eric, the smug poser, shouted, "You can run but you can't hide!" Lex slowed but kept going. He heard Eric laugh and say to the others, "Hey, I always wanted to say that!"

Lex glanced back at them. Daley looked like a tiger. She was right in Eric's face and, even at this distance, Lex heard every word she yelled: "Don't you *dare* say a word to anybody until we figure out what really happened!"

Eric backed away. He laughed again, and Lex heard him reply, "Yeah, sure. My lips are sealed."

Lex saw Daley mutter something to Nathan, and Nathan shook his head.

He could guess what they were saying.

Eric? His lips were sealed?

No. No way.

Not Eric.

Melissa sat in the girls' tent, brooding. The others talked about her. Of course they did. She knew that.

They always had. There was something about her, something she didn't particularly like, that attracted catcalls and sneers. Maybe that was why she always made an extra effort to be, well, *nice*.

Lot of good that did her. Everyone else at school seemed to belong to one clique or another—everyone had someone to hang out with.

Well, almost everyone. Jackson was still new, but with his kind of looks, he wouldn't have any trouble fitting in if he tried. He wouldn't be an outsider for long.

Not like me.

It was all Taylor's fault. She had watched Melissa's tape and then had taken such delight—such *evil* delight—in letting everyone know that Melissa liked Jackson.

Come on, Melissa told herself. *Taylor's not shy, like you. She didn't know how much her blabbing would hurt your feelings. Still—well, it did hurt.* And now with all the tapes missing, who knew—

From outside the tent came Taylor's excited yelp: "Hey! He's here! I got him!"

Melissa jumped up, opened the tent flap, and

stepped out into the windy day. Taylor was holding onto Lex's arm, and Lex looked absolutely frozen in surprise. Jackson and Eric came around the boys' tent and everyone zeroed in on Lex.

Melissa got to him first. Everything she had been feeling overflowed, and in an unusually spiteful tone—she was *never* spiteful—she heard herself demanding, "What were you thinking?" When Lex just gave her a silent, pleading look, she added, "Why did you take them?"

Lex tried to pull away from Taylor, but she kept her grip. She said, "Don't act all innocent with me!" When Lex didn't reply, she made her voice coaxing. Melissa winced at how fake Taylor sounded when she said, "Come on, Lex, just give me my tape. I don't care about the others, you can keep them—"

Jackson hunkered down, waving Taylor back. "It's cool, Lex."

Lex just gave him that wide-eyed, deer-in-the-headlights stare. Despite her irritation, Melissa felt a pang of sympathy. She knew what it was like to feel trapped when others were making fun of you, closing in on you.

With a sigh, Jackson said, "It'll be okay. Look, just give the tapes back and we'll forget all this."

But behind him, a grinning Eric crossed his arms in a gesture of triumph. "You can run—but you can't hide!"

Lex took a couple of faltering steps backward.

Daley came trotting up and stepped in front of him, protectively, as if shielding him from Melissa and the others. "Stop it!" she barked. Melissa saw Lex timidly creep behind her, as if terrified of what they might do to him. Daley reached a hand back and put it on his shoulder in a reassuring way. "You guys are too much," she said, shaking her head.

Taylor shrieked, "Us?"

Melissa darted her eyes toward Taylor. The blonde looked beside herself with disbelief, as if she couldn't understand Daley's defense of her brother. *Well, she can't understand much of anything.* Melissa blinked. Did she just think that? She, who never had a harsh word to say about anyone?

Taylor was looking around as if for support. "Hey, *he's* the one who took the tapes, the little creep! Daley's got no business yelling at us!"

A spasm of anger passed over Daley's face. "Hey! Don't call Lex names!"

Nathan stepped toward Eric, who uneasily backed away. In a low growl, Nathan said, "Way to keep it quiet, Eric. 'My lips are sealed.' Huh! Took you all of half an hour to unzip them."

"Just being a good citizen," replied Eric, as if he were the one under fire.

Melissa wanted to apologize to Lex for her harsh words. The poor kid looked half scared out of his wits. He peeked around from behind Daley.

Taylor held out her hand in an imperious way. "Hand 'em over, Peewee!"

Daley looked positively dangerous. "Taylor! Stop it! We don't even know that he took them."

Lex's face had turned scarlet. Melissa said, "Maybe—"

Taylor spun on her, as if Melissa had called her a name. *"Maybe what?"*

Inside, Melissa felt like shrinking away, like running off and hiding. She forced herself to stand her ground. "Maybe we should just ask him," she said softly.

It was a simple suggestion, but everyone looked a little surprised, as if that was the one thing they hadn't thought of. They all turned to stare at Lex, who faced them tensely.

Daley glanced at the others, and then she said, "Whatever you say, Lex, I'll believe you."

Taylor grumbled, "Speak for yourself!"

Daley snapped at her: "I just did! Now let him talk."

Lex looked from face to face, as if silently pleading with them. Melissa melted. Her irritation and anger seemed to have evaporated. The poor kid . . .

The wind ruffled Lex's dark hair. Miserably, he mumbled, "I . . . I don't know what to say." He shrugged. "I—I can't prove that I *didn't* take the tapes."

"See!" Taylor yelped with a note of triumph.

Then her eyes clouded over with a familiar mist of confusion. "Uh, wait," she said. She looked at Eric as if asking for his support. "Was that a confession?"

Melissa felt like blurting, "Leave him alone!" Except she had already used up her nerve.

Nathan looked pained, as though he had expected Lex to come up with a brilliant defense right on the spot. "Uh, Lex, I don't think it's possible to prove a negative. Is, uh, is that all you have to say?"

Lex nodded. Melissa saw Daley's expression and understood that she, too, felt torn—well, she would. Lex was part of her family, and families stuck together. If Lex had been Melissa's brother . . .

Eric was strutting around. "It's obvious he did it! I figured out that he was the only one—"

Nathan spun on him. "*You* figured it out? You were eavesdropping when—"

Eric spread his hands. "I came to an independent conclusion, okay? But that's not important now. The little rug rat did it, all right, but he's made it clear that he's not going to fess up and take responsibility. You know what we ought to do? I say we ought to have a trial!"

Melissa couldn't believe him. With some of the things Eric had gotten away with . . .

Daley actually laughed in Eric's face. "You can't be serious."

Eric crossed his arms but then had to make a wild grab as a gust nearly stole his straw hat again. Frowning as if annoyed by that, he asked, "Why not?"

"We're not lawyers or anything," Melissa pointed out timidly.

Eric gave her a wide grin. "No, but we're still civilized, right?" To the others, he said, "Look, as long as we're stuck here on the island, things like this are gonna happen, right?"

There was a general mutter of reluctant agreement.

Eric shrugged. "So I say we should figure out a way to deal."

Daley looked far from convinced. She shook her head. "Eric, that is so totally ridiculous."

"Really," Nathan said. Melissa remembered his confession—Nathan felt attracted to Daley. She frowned. The two of them had been together all morning, ever since the tapes had disappeared, as thick as—well, as thick as thieves. Could Nathan have guessed that Daley would like playing detective? Was that his way of getting close to her?

No one said anything for a long moment, but then Jackson stepped forward. "It's not ridiculous."

Melissa saw surprised glances snapping in Jackson's direction. The tall boy was unusually quiet, but when he spoke, people listened.

With a sigh, Jackson said, "We're all alone here. We have to make it work. No one else is gonna do that for us. We have to figure out a fair way to handle problems like this. A trial is a good idea."

Eric looked astonished. His voice actually squeaked: "It is?" He cleared his throat, and then pulled himself up to stand a little taller. "I mean, it is!"

But was it? Melissa wasn't sure. Daley threw a worried look toward Lex.

As for Lex—well, Melissa recognized his expression. It was one she had worn more than once.

Lex looked sick.

SEVEN

Eric had to admit that Jackson had surprised him. The big jerk must have a couple of brain cells to rub together after all. Of course the idea of a trial was brilliant. It was one of his!

Too bad he hadn't thought of appointing himself judge. That role would be played by Jackson, ladies and gentlemen. Still, well, the role of crusading prosecutor wasn't too shabby. There was that TV show where the prosecutor was practically the *star*, a man filled with righteous indignation.

Eric couldn't suppress a grin. Indignation he could do. As for righteousness, well, that could be faked.

He was eager to get started with this trial deal. They had dithered around as usual, hauling out an ice chest to serve as the judge's bench, and then Jackson had to find himself a short piece of tree limb with a knot in it to be his gavel.

They had even changed clothes. Jackson had put on a gray hooded warm-up jacket—well, the wind was kicking up, couldn't argue with that—and Nathan, like a copycat, had donned a similar one. Eric had decided on a black shirt edged with white; not exactly a three-piece suit, but a little more dignified than a bright blue T-shirt.

As for the ladies of the jury, well, Melissa had put on her light blue denim jacket, and Taylor wore a pink terry top.

And then, in her maroon jacket, there sat Daley, who had taken on the job of defending Lex. It was hard for Eric not to laugh at that. He would make mincemeat out of the little turkey. Wait— was mincemeat made of turkeys? It didn't matter. Daley, who always thought she knew everything, was in for a surprise.

She was up against a brilliant legal mind. His, in fact.

He studied the jury—Taylor, Nathan, and Melissa. Taylor, well, Taylor was a given. She already knew that the little sneak had taken the tapes. Why? Why, you ask?

Because I told her, that's why!

And Melissa, piece of cake, she'd go along with anybody just to avoid an argument. By the time Eric finished his examination of the witnesses, he could count on Taylor's vote and Melissa's.

That left Nathan. Nathan would vote against him, of course, no matter what. Eric supposed he was still ticked because Eric had claimed Nathan's little piece of detective work as his own.

Still, if he played his cards right, he might get Lex to confess to the theft, and then even Nathan would have to vote for conviction.

Hmm . . . what would be a good punishment? Eric hadn't thought of that. Then he felt a grin spreading across his face. The others had this nasty habit of expecting him to work—to do manual labor, when everyone could see he was an idea man.

Yes, it would be perfect. Lex would be sentenced to take over all the chores that Eric normally did. Beautiful. And then Eric would take Lex's place at the radio, listening for air traffic, sending out a distress call every once in a while, maybe tell a few jokes. What an easy—

Whoops. Jackson was rapping away at the ice chest with his stupid tree-branch gavel. The man was taking his role way too seriously. Jackson pinned down Eric with his dark, dangerous eyes. "Let's start this."

Play it cool. Show them how it's done. Eric picked up the coconut shell half full of water on the prosecution's desk—actually another one of the ice chests, a smaller one than his honor's—and made a bit of a production of taking a long drink of—ugh—warm water. Then he stood up, slowly. He grasped the lapels of his suit—well, anyway, he grasped the places on his shirt where lapels would have been if he'd been wearing a suit—and began to pace. "Thank you, your honor." Nicely done, deep baritone there, award-winning acting if you asked him.

He caught Daley rolling her eyes. *Roll away, girl. Hey, I'm on a roll myself!* He took his time, pacing back and forth in front of the jury. When you're on a roll, his dad had always told him, ride it for all it's worth.

Clearing his throat, Eric said, "Ladies and gentlemen—" Nathan was giving him that exasperated, get-on-with-it look— "ah, *gentleman* of the jury. The task before you today is a serious one, but not a difficult one. In fact, it's very simple. What we are looking for today is the truth. Nothing more, nothing less."

A worry line had appeared between Taylor's eyebrows. "I thought we were looking for the *tapes.*"

Eric sighed. Such a pretty package, and inside it was completely empty. But a prosecuting attorney couldn't alienate a juror, so he gave Taylor a little smile before continuing: "Today, by presenting a case that is absolutely ironclad, I intend to prove, beyond the shadow of a doubt—" Fast turn, arm raised like a cobra striking, an accusing finger of guilt pointing straight at a cowering Lex— "that

that man—uh, boy, kid, whatever—broke the sacred trust that binds us together!"

"Oh, brother." Nathan, the whiner of their discontent, in a whisper. Ignore him.

His voice rising dramatically, Eric said, "This individual, like a thieving, uh, thief, willfully and with reckless disregard for the laws which we all hold dear, while we unsuspectingly pursued our innocent pursuits, did creep into our—"

Bang! Jackson and his gavel. "Eric."

Irritation flickered as Eric broke off what was, let's all admit it folks, a brilliant opening statement. "Yeah, what?"

Deadpan, Jackson said, "Get over yourself."

For a moment he stood there, hearing the wind rattling the palm fronds overhead, their dry edges scratching against each other. Jackson had no sense of style. That was the problem when you let amateurs act.

"Fine," he said. He turned back to the jury. Maybe straight-from-the-shoulder honesty and bluntness would play here. "Lex took the tapes. I'm gonna prove it." He returned to the prosecutor's table—ice chest—and with mock courtesy he said to Daley, "Counselor?" He took his seat.

Jackson, improvising—you could always tell a bad actor by the quality of his ad-libs—said, "Go ahead, Daley." What a brilliant statement. The man should run for office. *Wait a minute—we already elected the chump.*

Daley was sitting beside Lex, who was looking down into his lap. Eric leaned toward them, wondering what kind of a defense Daley could possibly mount.

All she did was ask Lex, "Is there anything you want to say?"

Lex fiddled with the zipper of his tan jacket, raised his head, and his eyes met Eric's. The kid looked sullen. He said very clearly, "I'm innocent until proven guilty."

Ta-da! Ladies and gentlemen, you are about to vote this American defendant right into the penalty phase. Eric grinned at Lex, who looked defiant. *Proven guilty? My little weasel, that's exactly what I'm going to do!*

Daley drew a long, tired-sounding breath and stood up. Eric watched her. She wasn't really his type, too brainy and know-it-all, too sour, but she could really be kind of attractive if she'd only lighten up a little.

Daley was looking at the jurors. She said flatly, "I'm going to defend my brother and find the truth."

And then she sat back down.

Well, ladies and doofus of the jury, how was that? Not much of an opening statement, would you say? Sort of lacking in—everything. Eric stood up, dolefully shaking his head. Just to nail the point home, he said, "Not very stirring."

Jackson broke in again, sounding as if his

patience were starting to wear out: "Eric, where is the proof?"

Eric held out one hand as if asking for quiet. "Your honor, I now call to the witness stand—" *Big dramatic pause now, make them wait for it—* "Mr. Nathan McHugh!"

Jackson didn't sound impressed. "There is no stand. And Nathan happens to be in the jury. I think if Daley wanted to object—"

Whoa, whoa! Eric broke in: "Well, yeah, but it's not like we've got a whole lot of choices here!" He looked over at Daley, expecting her to follow Jackson's heavy hint and object, but she just sat there, shaking her head. Stupid decision, not what he would have done, but to each his own, right? "Your honor, since there are only seven of us here, I think we've gotta be a little loose with the rules."

Jackson just gave him that deadeye stare. Annoyance was flitting down under its surface, just like those fish that Jackson promised but never seemed to be able to deliver. Tightly, Jackson said, "Fine. Come on, Nathan."

Nathan sounded annoyed when he asked, "Can't I just stay here?"

Eric couldn't help heaving a dramatic sigh. He was up to his armpits in amateurs! "No," he said firmly. "When you're *there*, you're part of the jury." He pointed to a spot beside the judge's bench. Cooler. Whatever. "And when you're over *here*, then you're a witness. Do you understand the difference, or should I draw a little picture for you?"

With a glare, Nathan got up and crossed over to the spot where Eric was pointing. "All right, what do I do?"

"Just sit down." Jackson sounded like a dad telling the kids in the backseat to be quiet or he would turn that car right around.

Eric stepped forward. "Not yet. You sit after you've been sworn in." When Jackson flashed him a dirty look, he added, "We have to follow procedure. Your honor."

Jackson turned to Nathan. "Okay. You swear to tell the truth before this court, right?"

Nathan blinked at him. "Uh, yeah. I do."

"Fine. Then sit."

Gingerly, Nathan sat on the edge of the ice chest that was also the judge's bench. Eric stood looking sternly at him, then walked back over to his table and pretended to be scanning through an imaginary legal pad full of intricate notes. He couldn't keep a grin off his face when he overheard Taylor whispering to Melissa: "He's very good!"

With his arms behind his back, Eric slowly walked back toward Nathan, who was doing the eye routine again. *That's all right. I'll take that exasperated look right off your face, my man.*

"Mr. McHugh," Eric began in a grave voice,

"I will ask you to explain to the court, if you will, exactly why you think Lex took the tapes. Just tell us in your own words."

Nathan snorted. "Whose words do you think I'd use, you—"

"Your honor!" Eric said.

Jackson sighed. "Answer the question."

With a shake of his head, Nathan said, "I can't answer it. I mean, I don't even know if he really did take the tapes."

Eric couldn't believe his ears. "What! You said—I thought—" *Hold on there, partner. Don't lose your cool. Remember, you're Mr. District Attorney!* Smoothly, Eric said, "Let me rephrase the question, then, Mr. McHugh." He looked Nathan right in the eye. "Tell the court why you believe that Lex *may* have stolen the tapes."

Aha. Now Nathan squirmed, obviously uncomfortable under the scalpel-like sharpness of Eric's legal mind. "Well—" he began.

"We're waiting," Eric said sternly.

"Let him answer, Eric."

Nathan shrugged. "It's just that Daley and I tried to reconstruct what happened this morning."

Uh-oh. Taylor was looking lost. Eric cut in. "By reconstruct, you mean you were trying to figure out exactly what could have happened? Who would have had the chance to take the tapes, is that right?"

Frowning, Nathan said sarcastically, "Those

aren't my own words, but basically, yeah, that's right. Anyway, Daley and I tried to remember where everyone was between eight o'clock and ten o'clock—that's when the tapes had to be taken—and we could account for everyone but Lex."

"In other words, Mr. McHugh—"

"Lex was the only one in camp when the tapes were taken."

Even Taylor looked as if she'd understood that. But just in case any doubt was lingering up in that beautiful blond attic of hers, Eric turned dramatically and said, "Excuse me? You're telling the court that you actually determined this along with the defendant's own sister?"

"Yes."

"The defendant's *attorney*?"

"Look, Eric—"

"Yes or no, please."

"Yes!" Nathan practically spat the word out.

"In other words, you and Daley figured this out—and Daley has every reason to want to protect her little brother, and yet she still came to the conclusion that he's guilty! Guilty of this repulsive—"

Daley stood up. "Oh, give us a break, Eric!"

Eric gave her an ironic nod, then turned back to his witness. Nathan looked very uncomfortable now. "Uh, yeah," he admitted. "That's pretty much the way it is. But you have to understand—"

With a dismissive wave, Eric said, "Thank you, sir. I have no further questions. Ladies and witness—uh, I mean gentleman of the jury, the prosecution rests."

EIGHT

Daley couldn't believe Eric's performance. He was so full of himself, surely everyone could see that. But he had forced Nathan to that admission, and she had to admit she was about out of ideas.

She watched Eric strut back to his ice chest and sit down with an elaborate air of smugness.

And to her annoyance, she heard Taylor murmur again to Melissa: "He's really very good."

Jackson gave her a pitying sort of glance, but then he turned to Eric and said, "The prosecution rests? That's it?"

Eric nodded. "What else do you want? Lex was the only one with an opportunity to take the tapes. He took 'em. End of story." He sat. "I'll reserve the rest for my closing instructions to the jury."

"The judge gives the instructions," Jackson said. "You can make a closing argument."

"Fine. Whatever."

Wearily, Jackson said, "Okay. Go ahead, Daley."

Daley gave Lex a sideways glance. He wouldn't meet her eyes. "Hey," she whispered to him. "Last chance."

Lex shrugged and shook his head. To Daley he looked about half his real age at the moment. He looked like a five-year-old who'd been caught with his hand in the cookie jar.

Guilty, in fact.

But she had to make some kind of defense. She stood up and said, "I don't have any questions for Nathan."

Nathan got up and returned to the jury, sitting next to Taylor, who edged away from him.

Daley said, "I'd like to bring Lex up."

Lex sighed and started to stand.

Daley said, "You can sit where you are, Lex. We don't really have a witness stand."

"But swear him in!" Eric said. "Your honor, I object—"

"Oh, be quiet," Jackson said. "Lex, tell the truth, okay?"

In a small voice, Lex said, "Okay."

Eric sprang to his feet, but at a sharp glance from Jackson, he sat down again, mumbling, "Good enough."

Daley remembered the hard job of running for office back in school. You had to get people on your side, and to do that you had to do more than just ask questions.

Besides, she remembered one of the movies her dad had made, a movie about an attorney who lost an important case. What had the woman said? "Never ask a witness a question if you don't already know the answer."

Well, she didn't know what Lex might say. So—

Daley turned toward the jury and said, "We have our differences. We've all made mistakes and said stupid things, right?"

Taylor's eyes snapped. "Hey, are you calling me *stupid*?"

Nathan shushed her. "She's saying *everyone's* been stupid sometimes."

"Oh," Taylor said. "Okay, then."

Daley sighed. "Yes, I mean we've all done and said things we wish we could change. But when things get serious, we know we can rely on each other. That's why we've come this far, why we've survived. Right, Lex?"

Lex was looking worried, as if he wasn't sure where this was going. Well, that made two of them. Lex nodded and said, "Uh, yeah. Right."

Daley wished she could read minds. Nathan was leaning forward, his eyes intense on Lex. Melissa's expression was troubled. Taylor just looked a little grumpy. Daley continued, "Now, the videotapes were a good idea of Nathan's. They were a way of releasing the pressure when the stress started to get to us. We knew we could talk to the camera and whatever we said was going to be private. Totally private."

"Like a diary!" Taylor said brightly. She turned to Melissa. "There was this one time, my mom read my diary and—"

Jackson rapped his gavel. "Later, Taylor. Right now you just listen."

Taylor made a face at him.

Daley turned to Lex. "Anyway, the point is the videos were, as Taylor says, like a diary. They needed to be absolutely private, right, Lex?"

"Yup." Good. He at least sounded confident, whatever he was feeling. Daley saw that she had their interest. Everyone, even Eric, seemed to be hanging on Lex's words.

Daley said, "But we all know that the only way it could work was if we were on the honor system. Nobody was supposed to watch anyone else's tape. And it worked, except for one unfortunate incident."

Melissa turned an accusing eye toward Taylor, who tossed her head and muttered, "Hey, if you can't take a joke—"

"It's all right," Melissa said in a low voice.

Daley resumed. "Well, except for just that once, we've all held to that honor system. Right, Lex?"

Lex looked up at her. She could see puzzlement in his eyes, but also trust. "Yeah," he said. "That's right."

Raising her voice over the background roar of surf and wind, Daley said, "But now we're all worried that our honor system has fallen down."

"Because that little rat has no honor!" Eric said, pointing at Lex.

"Hang on!" Jackson said, but they were all talking at once.

Nathan stood up. "Quiet!" They fell silent at his sudden shout. "We've *got* to trust each other! Daley's right—this is important. If we don't trust each other, we're gonna die out here."

"Over a camera?" Taylor asked.

"Over matters of life and death," Nathan said. "We have to depend on each other for food, shelter, survival—but if we can't even trust each other on little things, we're sure not going to do it over big ones! So, yes, we have to trust each other even on stuff as small as the camera!"

Daley raised her voice: "That's a great point, Nathan. Thanks." She took a step toward the judge's bench and picked up the camera. "Now, here's something that I just don't get. We don't want anyone watching those tapes—but no one is. I found the camera in its container, right where it's always been. Nobody took it."

Eric was on his feet. "Nobody's accused Lex

of stealing the camera! He just took the tapes, the little sneak!"

"Come on, Eric!" Daley waved the camera. "Think for a second! What use are the tapes by themselves? We don't have a video player—the only way to watch the tapes is to use the camera! So if someone stole the tapes to watch them, why didn't they take the camera, too? Get it? You can't watch the tapes without the camera!"

Taylor stood up. "Hey, she's right!"

"Great point!" Nathan said.

Melissa said hesitantly, "But why take the tapes, then?"

Putting the camera back down, Daley said, "I think that whoever took the tapes *didn't* want to watch them."

"Objection!" Eric yelled. "A theory isn't evidence!"

Jackson pointed his gavel at Eric. "You keep quiet." He turned toward Daley. "And you—keep going."

Daley had the feeling she was way out on thin ice, but she had to go ahead. "The only thing that makes sense to me is the idea that the thief wasn't looking for secrets at all, but trying to hide one."

Eric snorted. "That's ridiculous. Look, if somebody didn't want a secret to come out, they would never have said anything on a tape about it, that's all."

"I didn't say it was the thief's *own* secret," Daley pointed out.

The others whispered together, but she plowed on: "Look, I think the thief took the tapes because one of them had a secret on it that no one should ever see. Whatever that secret is, it would have to be so bad that somebody was willing to become a thief and—"

"But they'd just have to take the one tape," Nathan said.

"No. Think. If one person's tape was gone, we'd know who had the secret. But if all the tapes are gone, then the thief has covered his tracks."

"*His* tracks?"

"Or hers. Whatever."

Funny, but now that she was into it, Daley could see how everyone was struggling to look innocent—Melissa, Taylor, Eric, even Nathan. None of them wanted her looking too closely at their faces as she paced around. "So the real question becomes this: Who has something on their video that is so bad it would be a disaster if everybody found out?"

Melissa couldn't meet her gaze. She was blushing furiously.

Daley continued. "I'm not talking about having a crush on someone. It has to be something more serious than that. At least one person knows: the thief. But I think I know who the thief is, and I guarantee that there couldn't be anything on that person's video that could be bad enough to cause all this. That means that the thief took the videos to cover for somebody else."

She looked back and said softly, "Right, Lex?"

Lex almost moaned. "Yes," he said unwillingly. "You're right."

Everyone erupted: "Yes!" "No!" "What?" "Lex took them?"

From their voices, Daley sensed a change in their attitudes—they were surprised, astonished, but not angry. No one seemed in a mood to punish Lex.

Eric was waving his arms. "I knew it! I knew it! He's guilty as charged, ladies and—"

But now Lex had jumped up, too, clenching his hands at his sides and looking angry. "Yeah, I took them!"

"Ha!" Eric said. "He admits—"

"I took them!" Lex repeated, his voice rising in fury. "But I took them to keep them away from *you*, Eric!"

Daley looked at the prosecutor. Eric's mouth opened and closed. Fleetingly, she thought he looked like a fish out of water. Finally, feebly, he squeaked, "Me?"

Jackson pounded away with his gavel.

Lex looked so miserable that Daley was wondering if she had just wrecked her little brother's life.

Through his anger, Lex heard Jackson

pounding away for silence. "Easy!" he yelled. "Easy, everyone! Back off!"

And they all fell silent. Well, almost all of them.

Taylor was shaking her head. "I am so confused!"

Jackson pointed toward Lex with his gavel. "Just pay attention for a minute, okay? I think we should give him a chance to talk, everyone. We're going to be fair with this. What's the story, Lex?"

Lex's face felt burning hot. This was just what he'd been trying to avoid. But now he was in a corner—

Daley said, "Come on, Lex. It's over. You have to tell us."

Making an effort to control his breathing, to make his heart stop hammering so hard, Lex said, "Okay. Yesterday I saw something that—that I shouldn't have seen."

They were all leaning toward him.

Lex took another deep breath and remembered how it had been . . .

They'd just found Abby, but she was dehydrated and weak. She'd recovered a little—she kept drinking water, and she was finally able to sit up, able to talk.

While the bigger kids were talking to her, Lex

decided it would be good to bring some more water in. He picked up a plastic container that would hold a gallon, so heavy that it would be hard for him to lug once it was full, but that was okay, he could rest, it didn't have to be one long haul. He was on his way to the well, empty container swinging at his side. The path took him up the hill, past a thick tangle of brush.

No one else was around. No sound but the chattering and chirping of birds, the background buzz of insects, the far-off crash of surf on the reef.

And then, crouching behind a stand of trees as if he were hiding—

Lex said, "I saw Eric watching somebody else's videotape."

Eric gave him a long blank look. "What? You were *spying* on me?"

Taylor squinted at him. "Eric? But he *made* my tape, he didn't have to—"

"It wasn't yours," Lex said reluctantly.

Nathan was looking ticked off. "I knew Eric had something to do with this."

Daley said, "Go ahead, Lex."

Something about the way Eric was sitting, crouched over, looked suspicious. Setting the water container carefully down, Lex crept up behind Eric. It was easy—Eric was bending forward, totally fixated on the camera, listening to the tinny little voice coming out of the miniature speaker. He was even chuckling to himself as he watched, as if he were enjoying a good comedy on TV.

But when Eric laughed, it usually meant trouble for someone else.

So Lex sneaked up on him without his noticing. He could see the little liquid-crystal screen on the camera, and with a shock he realized that Eric must have taken someone else's video diary. He recognized the face, the voice.

For a few minutes he just stood there, staring over Eric's shoulder, not believing what he was hearing.

"I—I watched some of the tape, too," Lex confessed. "It was wrong. I mean, I was as bad as Eric. And I saw something on the tape that no one was supposed to see."

Eric waved his arms. "Aren't we gonna *punish* this little rat? I mean, he was invading my privacy, looking right over my shoulder! The little sneak!"

"Eric," Daley said.

"And he lied!" Eric went on. "He said he was innocent until we proved him guilty, but he was guilty all—"

Daley spun on him and roared, "Sit down and shut up!" Lex felt a small ripple of satisfaction at the stunned look on Eric's face as he flopped back down. One thing about Daley, when she'd had it with you, she let you know it!

She said to Lex, "All right. I think you're going to have to tell us now. What did you see?"

Lex looked down at his hands, struggling with his conscience. Finally, he said, "No. I won't tell you that. It was private."

"Lex—"

He gave his sister an exhausted look. "It would be wrong, Day. Look, I could hear Eric laughing about what he was seeing. You all know how he is—he can't keep quiet if he can get someone else in trouble. I knew he was gonna tell everybody what he had seen, just the same way he told everybody what you and Nathan figured out about who must have taken the tapes. And he'd conveniently forget to tell everyone that it started when *he* stole someone else's tape."

"Well," Eric huffed. "Obviously, some things are more important than the letter of the law, like civic duty—"

No one paid him any attention. Lex shrugged. "Okay, so you're right about me. The thing is, I figured that if the video was missing, then no matter what Eric said, he wouldn't have any proof to back him up. So I took the tape when I got a chance, and then I realized that the person would worry about someone watching it. So I took all of them. That way, no one would know who had the secret, and everyone would be in the same boat. I'm sorry."

"But what you saw—"

Lex stubbornly shook his head. "No. It was private."

Daley said, "There's one other person who *can* tell us."

They all looked at Eric.

NINE

Eric was sweating, despite the gusty wind. If he'd had any idea that this was all about the tape he'd watched, he would have covered his tracks! The jury wasn't supposed to turn against the prosecutor! The prosecutor was the one who crusaded for justice, for truth, and all that junk! But if they knew what he knew—

Wait. That was it.

"All right," he said, making a big show of reluctance. *Maybe I could tell them I was gonna record my own video, and one was left in—no, they'd never buy that. Have to take another approach, one they'd never expect from him.* "Yes, yes, it's true. I did watch a tape. Okay, so I'm the bad guy!"

They were all grumbling at him now, looking outraged that he would make such an admission.

But he raised his voice: "Look, it was just curiosity, okay?"

"Wait," Taylor said. "Are you saying that you, like, *stole* someone's video?"

"Yes! I admit it," Eric told her. "I'm sorry, everyone. And I probably shouldn't have done it. I was just curious, that's all—I mean, we have to be together on this island, and I sort of wanted to know something about who I'm sharing it with, so, yeah, I watched a stupid tape. But, hey, if you've got something to hide, why put it on a video, right? I mean, why run the risk of somebody seeing your worst secret by accident, or even on purpose? And you know what? I'm glad I got curious! Because I discovered a secret about someone!"

"What was it?" Taylor asked. "Something stupid, I'll bet. Is Daley in love with Nathan or something?"

Eric saw Nathan blush and quickly look down at his feet. Daley just frowned at Taylor's question. Eric shook his head and replied, "Nothing as simple as that. No, it's bad." He made his voice deeper, more dramatic: "In fact, the terrible truth is that this one person's secret could put us all in danger!"

They were all quiet now, all of them staring at him. And a certain someone, the one whose tape he had watched, would be sweating. The others— well, the others were hooked!

Good, I've got their attention. Now they're not

wondering about me any longer, but about the one with the deep, dark secret.

Okay, don't just hand it to them on a silver platter or anything. Make 'em ask for it. Make 'em beg.

He said, "I can live with the secret, I guess. Though it might mean risking my life—risking all of our lives, in fact. Yes, it's that bad, people. But you have to ask yourselves something now. Do you really want me to keep a dangerous secret from you all? Or do you want to know?" He had them, he could tell. Even Nathan was looking curious. Humbly, he added, "I'll do whatever you think is right. I just want to help, that's all."

Lex looked stunned. "No! You can't!"

"Hey, I want to know if I'm in some kind of danger," Taylor said. "That makes sense. Right?"

No one answered her.

Lex was pleading now: "Don't say anything else, Eric. Just stop talking, okay? You're not—"

Daley cut in. "Eric, you've just said you took someone else's video. In my book, that makes you just as guilty as Lex. In fact, you're worse than he is, because he was trying to protect someone."

"That's just what I'm trying to do," Eric protested. "Okay, maybe what I did was wrong, but I didn't mean anything by it. But now, knowing as much as you do, tell me what's more important? Secrecy—or safety?"

Lex turned to the others. "Listen, Eric doesn't know the whole story!"

"I know more than you, squirt! Hey, by his own admission, Lex just saw a little part of the video. I saw the whole thing. The whole thing!"

Eric could tell that Lex was getting frustrated. "You're making too big a thing out of this!"

"Am I?" All innocence, all surprise, that was the right note to hit. *Look at them, hanging on my every word. And one of them is squirming because one of them knows what the secret must be.* Eric lowered his voice to a confidential level. "When I looked at that tape, I learned something about one of us that—well, I'll be honest. It scared me. I think it would scare everybody. Don't you want to know the rest?"

Jackson snapped, "Don't answer him, anybody," he said. "Just say it, Eric."

Sweet!

"All right," Eric said, very slowly. "The secret I discovered was about—"

He whirled and stabbed an accusing finger.

"—*you*, Jackson!"

"What?" Melissa yelped.

"Eric, that's mean!" Lex yelled. The others had all jumped to their feet, all except Jackson. Eric grinned at him, enjoying the blank, stunned look in Jackson's eyes.

"Well?" he asked quietly. "Jackson? Don't you think it's time you told us the truth?"

TEN

Jackson had long ago learned it was better never to let his emotions show in his face. That's what they wanted you to do, all the teachers, the social workers, even the police. People like them pinned you down with their sharp eyes and then watched you for a telltale sign of weakness, a sign of feeling, and then they pounced on it and used it against you.

So when Eric spun around and made his dramatic accusation and the others gasped, Jackson didn't flinch at all. Solid as a rock, don't show any weakness. He lowered his head and gave Eric an empty, cold glare. If you didn't give them an opening, they couldn't get at you.

But Jackson felt something rising inside him, something cold and bitter. All the trouble was about to begin all over again, everything that he'd thought was behind him. He could sense it slouching back into his life. All the distrust, all the fear, all the empty sense of loss and betrayal.

Taylor, from her spot in the jury box, was gazing at Jackson with a sort of dim wonder in her eyes. "Uh—what was it that he said on the video?"

Eric, standing there with the wind ruffling his brown hair, his head thrown back, a look of challenge on his smug face, said, "Watch the tape and you'll find out just how bad it really is."

Lex jumped up. He looked really distressed, as upset as Jackson had ever seen him, and he sounded furious when he burst out, "No!" He turned in a tight circle, as if appealing to everyone at once. "Don't you see? That's exactly why I took the tapes away and hid them, so that nobody could watch them! This is just wrong, Eric! It's not our business!"

Daley put her calming hand on Lex's shoulder and added her defiant voice to his. "Lex is absolutely right. It doesn't matter what's on the tape, Eric. It's private. They're *all* private, remember?"

Eric was on the edge of the group, keeping a careful distance. His eyes kept cutting toward Jackson, though, anxiously flicking toward the gavel, as if he were half afraid Jackson would nail him with it. He said, "This is a trial, right?" He looked around as if expecting confirmation, but no one answered him. He nodded and answered himself: "Yeah, this is a trial. So I say let's leave it up to the jury." He didn't fully turn to face them—from where he stood, that would have meant turning his back to Jackson—but he sidled toward the jury box and asked, "How do you vote? For safety? Or for secrets?"

The question hung heavy in the air. Jackson felt something inside him sink. No one would meet his eyes.

He was losing them. He could see the worried glance pass between Melissa and Nathan, the two most reasonable members of the jury, and Taylor was still staring at him with her mouth hanging open and her face screwed up as if she thought she had missed something important but couldn't quite make out exactly what that might have been.

I could let them decide, but how can they go any way but the way Eric has taken them? And afterward, how will they feel, turning against the guy they elected leader? How will they ever trust each other again after that? No. I can't have that on my conscience.

No. You took responsibility for your own life. If he had to go down in flames, he'd rather call the shot himself.

"Lex," he said, a little surprised at how steady his voice sounded. He didn't *feel* steady inside. He felt as if he was about to lose something vastly important.

Lex was trembling. He knew. He had seen the video, or the most important part of it, judging from what he had said in his testimony. "What?"

Jackson meant to smile, but somehow he couldn't get his face to make the expression. "I appreciate what you did," he told Lex, keeping his voice quiet. "But it's over. Go get my videotape."

Poor Lex looked as if Jackson had screamed at him, had threatened to hit him. He actually flinched. "Jackson? No!"

"Yeah," Jackson said. The sun went behind a cloud, and he felt the odd chill of the sudden shadow. Funny how even here in the tropics you could all at once feel cold like that. "Lex, go get it."

For a few heartbeats, Jackson was sure Lex would defy him. The little kid clenched his hands into fists, braced himself as if to resist, to stand his ground—but then he dropped his gaze, shook his head, and turned away. He ran off clumsily, as if his feet had suddenly become too heavy for him, head down, not even looking where he was going. Jackson thought, *Poor little guy. This is as hard for him as it is for me. Harder, maybe.*

"Hey," Eric said. "Can we trust him?"

Daley sounded as if she'd had just a little bit more than enough. "Eric, shut up!"

"I'm going to follow him," Eric announced. "Lex was sneaky enough to take the tapes and almost get away with it. I don't want him to destroy

Jackson's before you have a chance to see it."

Jackson didn't respond. He was just as glad to see Eric trot off.

Off at sea a sudden streak of lightning fractured the dark roil of clouds, and an instant later a loud crash of thunder rolled in, making even Jackson jump in his skin. His head whipped around.

How had the cloud bank crept in so close, how had it turned that ugly gray-purple, low and menacing and as nasty as a bad bruise?

He heard Nathan's shaky voice. "Something's coming."

Yeah.

Jackson could feel it, too.

Something *bad* was coming.

Melissa hugged herself, as if trying to hold warmth inside her body. The day had turned bleak and dark, and not just from the rack of cloud that had slid across the face of the sky. They all stood near the downed plane. Lex had returned their tapes, Eric dogging him all the way.

Lex had suggested that if they all absolutely had to watch, they could all hear the sound track a lot better if he hooked the camera up to the mp3 speaker system they had used to provide music for the dance. God, was that just last night? It seemed a week ago, a lifetime ago.

So Lex had clambered up the side of the plane on his homemade, lashed-up wooden ladder and was busily plugging a cable into the speakers. He came back down and bent to plug the other end into the video camera.

Thunder rumbled again, sounding like a heavy ball trundling across an uneven wooden floor, as if a giant were bowling with a misshapen stone. Melissa winced at the prolonged roar, though it was farther away than that first startling crash. She raised her head to stare up at the threatening sky, a frightening dark gray festooned with hanging, drifting pouches of even darker cloud seething off in the distance.

As the last rolling grumble died, Taylor said in her complaining, whiny voice, "I hate thunder."

Nathan looked as edgy as Melissa felt, his eyes jumpy, his movements jerky. He pushed his long hair out of his face and said, "Don't be afraid of thunder. It's just noise. It's the lightning you've got to worry about."

Not just the lightning, Melissa thought. They had more than that to worry about at the moment. Jackson was standing off by himself, toward the tail of the plane, silent and as immovable as a statue.

"Come on, Lex," nagged Eric, leaning over the smaller boy's shoulder. "Can't we please just do this?"

Lex shot him an angry look. Melissa stepped

forward. "Hey, Lex, just play the part Eric's talking about. Nothing else."

"You're gonna miss some juicy bits," taunted Eric.

"Gotcha," Lex said to Melissa. "Just let me cue up the tape."

Daley had pulled up the hood of her maroon workout jacket, though the rain was still holding off. She looked back toward Jackson, and the wind caught and ballooned her hood for a moment. She swiped it down and asked, "Do you want to say anything first?"

Jackson didn't move. "Why?"

Melissa winced. Did he have to be so—so macho? Surely whatever it was couldn't be all that bad. Maybe it was even a misunderstanding, a mistake. Most things could be explained if you just gave the person half a chance—

"Okay," Lex said. "It's ready. Everyone close in so you can see."

Nathan, Daley, and Taylor crowded close. Melissa hung back, trying to catch Jackson's eye, to give him at least a reassuring nod. He didn't seem to notice her, but Eric did. He waggled his eyebrows at her, teasingly. Melissa wanted to scream at him to stop it.

Only—no. Melissa never screamed.

Along with the others, she watched the small screen as Jackson appeared, just his head and shoulders showing in a tight close-up. The cross medallion that he wore gleamed dully against the top of his dark T-shirt. He was looking directly into the camera's eye, seeming to look right at Melissa, as he spoke in an even voice:

Jackson

... I feel pretty much alone on this island. My head's not in the same place as the others'.

Jackson paused, but his calm gaze never dropped away from the camera. He appeared to think for a moment before continuing. Melissa felt sorry for him. He seemed so—alone.

Truth is, I'm in no big hurry to be rescued.

He shrugged. His voice was light enough, but he didn't crack a smile.

I mean, it's not like I want to eat coconuts for the rest of my life, but realistically, what have I got to go back to? They won't let me see my mom. The foster home is fine. I mean, they treat me okay there, but it's not home. That high school they've got me going to is full of spoiled rich kids.

He took another thoughtful pause and gave a resigned sigh that made Melissa's heart ache. She knew what it was like to be the odd one out in a crowd.

After that guy was hurt the night before we left, well, I knew then that I was in trouble.

Yeah, I can pretty much guarantee they would've shipped me back to juvie hall if we hadn't left on this trip.

On the screen, Jackson's image took on a defiant look.

But whatever happens, I'm not going back there. At least here they can't get to me. And the longer I stay away, well, the better it will be. If I'm out of reach, then things will have more of a chance to cool down back there and—

"That's enough." Melissa, surprisingly, took a step forward, reached out, and switched off the camera.

Melissa couldn't believe that she had worked up the nerve to do that, but Jackson had seemed so unhappy in the tape, so hopeless—

Taylor had her hand up to her mouth. Her eyes were wide with shock and disbelief. "Omigod! Did you *hear* that?"

Nathan nodded, the same way a kindergarten teacher would nod to a little kid having a moment of anxiety. "We all heard it, Taylor. Okay, who got hurt?"

"Doesn't matter!" Eric crowed immediately. Melissa ground her teeth together at the sound of his self-satisfied voice. "Point is, our mystery man is bound for jail because he hurt somebody! Yeah, he's headin' for the slammer, for stir, for the big lockup, for the pen, for—"

"Shut up," Daley said. "Can that be true?"

"You heard him!" Eric shot back. "Of course it's true. He said it himself, and we have his confession on tape!"

Melissa was tired of Eric's playing prosecutor. "Hey," she said, "we should at least give him a chance to explain. Jackson—"

But he was gone. Somehow he had simply faded away from his spot back toward the tail of the plane. Melissa felt a jolt as she saw that nothing was there now but the empty beach, and then the choppy lagoon, and then the ocean, dark and threatening under the heavy sky. Lightning reached down on the far horizon, dipping a white-hot toe in the tossing, turbulent water.

Taylor, her hand still hiding her mouth, was sounding close to hysterical. "Omigod!" she blurted again. "Did everyone *hear* that? Did you hear what he *said*? I am so not a spoiled rich kid!"

Everyone exchanged glances, and Melissa thought, *That's Taylor for you. Always thinking of number Taylor.* She immediately grimaced, feeling guilty for just having thought that.

Eric slapped the side of the plane, making a hollow boom. "We have to face it, boys and girls. We are living on a small island with a dangerous criminal who doesn't even want to get rescued." He grimaced in a malicious, evil sort of way. "And what did we do? We made him the boss! Real smart move, you guys!"

Melissa was shaking with anger now. "Come on, Eric. We don't know—"

"You heard him! How would you explain it? He's a pretty poor prospect for a boyfriend now, wouldn't you say?"

Melissa felt herself blushing. "Jackson's a—he's a troubled guy."

Eric reeled around the beach, his arms flapping as if he were trying to take off in the stiffening breeze and fly away. "Troubled? *Troubled*? We're *all* troubled! Me, I'm troubled about being stuck here with a criminal!"

Melissa couldn't trust herself to speak. She took deep breaths.

"We don't know enough about this," Nathan was insisting. "And I think Melissa's right. We owe Jackson a chance to—"

"Owe him?" Eric said, his sneering tone adding to Melissa's frustration and irritation. "Will you listen to yourself? We weren't the ones to keep our criminal pasts secret—he was! I don't think we owe him a thing!"

Daley took a quick step in Eric's direction, and

he fell back. "So what do you suggest we do, Eric? Should we lock Jackson up? For what? He didn't do anything to us!"

"Yet," Taylor said, to Melissa's annoyance. She thought, *Is that how the law works? Lock someone up because he might do something wrong? Great, we'd all be in prison!*

Eric beamed at her and gave Daley a smirk.

Thunder crashed again, from close by, and the wind whipped up. Melissa tasted salt on her lips. The incoming wind was scooping the tops off waves, shattering the water into a fine, needlelike spray. It stung her eyes, and she turned away from it, feeling the gusts buffeting her back, like a big, playful dog jumping up on her.

Except this didn't feel playful at all.

"Come on," Nathan said, his voice full of concern. "We'd better get to higher ground. The storm's coming closer."

A streak of lightning glared from what felt like only a few feet overhead, and a blast of thunder made the ground shake underfoot.

"I think," Melissa heard her own panicky voice say, "it's already here."

ELEVEN

The worst of the storm hung low in the sky, out at sea. Raging wind tore at the waves, and the cloud cover trailed in long, ragged wisps. Barrages of thunder rolled in from the ocean.

So far only the edge of the storm brushed the island. Daley watched it nervously as she lugged gear into the boys' tent. If only the storm didn't change its track—but they couldn't count on that. She went back for another load.

She had just emerged from the girls' tent again when Lex came up, holding a stack of videotapes. He watched her enter the boys' tent, then come out again empty-handed. "What are you doing?"

"Putting all the gear in one tent to make room," Daley explained. "So we can all ride out the storm together."

Lex nodded. "Oh."

She ducked into the girls' tent again and came out with one of the plastic containers. Lex still stood there. She smiled at him. "Want to help?"

"Uh, sure. Could—could you do me a favor?"

"Sure, what?"

Lex held out the stack of stolen videos. "Could you give these back to everybody?"

"No problem," Daley told him. "You can put them in here." She set the container down, popped the lid, and they stowed the tapes. "I'll give them back," Daley said, "but I don't think anyone's worried about the videos anymore."

"Tell everyone I'm sorry I took them," Lex blurted. He looked miserable. "It's just that I was afraid Eric would—would do exactly what he did. He turned everybody against Jackson."

"It's okay," Daley said. "Nobody is mad at you."

Lex sniffled. "He's a good guy, Day."

Is Jackson a good guy? Daley wished she knew. "I think he is," she said slowly. "But you have to admit, what he said on the video was kind of scary. And we don't really know him."

Together they moved everything loose into the boys' tent, then moved sleeping bags from the boys' to the girls'. Daley wrinkled her nose. Didn't these guys *bathe* before they climbed into the bags? Well, none of them were going to win any awards for being well groomed.

But that isn't the question. The question is—what

is Jackson really like? He didn't say much, but he worked hard. And since he didn't talk a lot, he didn't complain. Point in his favor. Still—

Daley wondered how much of her uncertainty came from the fact that everyone except Nathan and her—well, and Jackson, to be fair—had voted for Jackson as leader. She wasn't used to losing, and the thought that the other four would vote for him even though he wasn't actually running sort of galled her.

Still, Jackson had contributed a lot to their survival so far, and when he did speak, he made sense and laid down rules that she had to agree with. He was the one who insisted they all had to work. Eric couldn't coast along on being an "idea man," as he called it. And Jackson worked as hard as any of them. Harder. You had to give him that.

The trees were lashing in the wind now, the taller ones bending far over. Leaves and even small branches whipped off as the gusts slammed into the island. Another sizzling bolt of lightning seared the dark cloud, too close for comfort, and thunder hammered the earth.

Lex flinched and muttered, "That's not good."

Taylor couldn't understand why the steady wind didn't cool things off. The clouds were really heavy off at sea, so dark they were almost black.

Gray curtains of rain swept over the face of the ocean. Funny, it was still dry as a bone here on the beach.

And *hot*. Even the wind blasting in felt muggy, humid, soggy, stifling. She'd give anything for a quick dip right now.

Except you weren't supposed to go swimming during a thunderstorm. Or was it that you weren't supposed to stand under a tree? Or maybe swim under a tree? Or was it that you weren't supposed to swim if there was a thunderstorm and you'd just eaten? One of those things. Better play it safe. But you could wade, so she sloshed along through the shallow water. As usual, Eric was close by, walking on the beach just a few feet away.

Above the roar of the wind, Taylor asked, "So is Jackson like some . . . bad guy? The video was so confusing. But I'm not sure I even want to be around him anymore."

Eric kept stooping to pick up seashells. He flung them out into the lagoon with a sidearm pitch, trying to make them skip, but the water was pretty choppy. Most of them hit with a *splunk!* and vanished at once. "I don't wanna be around him, either," Eric said. "But face it, this is an island. It's not like we have a whole lot of choice."

With a frown, Taylor watched him pick up another shell and toss it. He actually got one skip out of that one. Why wasn't he paying attention?

She had an important question: "But should he even be our leader?"

"Huh?"

"On the video he said he doesn't even want to get rescued," Taylor explained patiently. "But wasn't that the whole point? I thought we were electing a leader that would help us get rescued. If he doesn't want that, should Jackson be our leader?"

"No," Eric said.

"So what do we do now?"

"Well," Eric said slowly, "we have to elect somebody new, somebody who can come up with the right kind of ideas to find a way to get us off this island."

"Like Daley or Nathan?"

Eric put his hands on his hips and stood tall. "No," he said again, his voice so serious that Taylor gave him a sharp look. He had to grab for his hat, which the wind was trying to steal, but once he had his hand on it, he said, "The leader should be me. Me, Taylor. That's who."

The wind had just risen to a moaning blast, and a wave had crashed just as Eric spoke. Taylor couldn't help laughing. "What? I'm sorry. For a second I thought you said the leader should be— you."

Eric's expression was offended. "Why not?" he demanded.

"Why not? Because you're not—well, not Jackson!"

"Wasn't I the guy who exposed the criminal?" Eric asked her.

"But Jackson was the one who recorded the tape, and he more or less just *said*—"

"But didn't I smoke out the video thief?"

"Huh? You mean Lex? I thought it was Nathan and Daley who—"

"Most of all," Eric said, sounding really upset with her, "didn't I stay cool under pressure?"

Taylor rolled her eyes and took one more sloshing step. All at once it felt as if she had stepped on a live electric wire. Pain surged up from her left foot, a blinding, stabbing, incredible pain. She staggered and screamed, *"Aahhh!"*

Eric jumped about a foot. "Taylor? What's wrong?"

Air hissed between Taylor's clenched teeth as she stood on one foot. The worst pain passed, but her whole foot still throbbed. She looked down in the water but couldn't see any blood. "It hurts," she moaned. "I stepped on a sharp rock or something, and—*oww!*" She had to put down her foot to keep her balance. Putting her weight on her left heel, she tried to wade ashore. "Help me, please!"

Eric was backing away. "You cut your foot? Look, I sort of have a problem with blood, but I'll go and get help—"

"No!" Taylor said. She was out of the water now, and everything *looked* to be in one piece.

Her toes were all there, and only a trickle of blood dripped from the sole of her foot. "Eric, don't you dare run away! Come here and help me."

Eric took a few tentative steps forward. "Oh, yeah. Uh, right. Sure."

Taylor couldn't believe this. She needed to lean on his shoulder, needed to put her arm around him for support, and he was acting like she had the *plague* or something—*oh, God, it hurt again!* "Just stand still," she groaned, waiting for another wave of pain to pass. *Oh, it was bad, it hurt so much!*

Gasping for air, Taylor shivered as, for the first time, the thought hit her: *I could die on this island!*

TWELVE

At the plane, Lex climbed up his ladder onto the wing. The weather was turning even more blustery and threatening. A steady, strong onshore wind now thrummed and hummed against the plane's surfaces. His jerry-rigged antenna, raised up on a bamboo pole, quivered and sang in the wind.

Looked like a lot of rain out at sea, heavy rain, dark and gray, and moving fast. Better move the radio somewhere dry. He began to disconnect it from the antenna.

At first he thought the shriek came from the wind, but then he realized it had been a girl yelling. Lex jumped down and ducked around the front of the plane. Far down the beach, he saw Taylor's pink-clothed form splashing out of the water. Eric put an arm around her.

Great, Lex thought. *They've been playing, probably splashing each other. That's probably why Taylor is squealing like a little baby—*

No, wait. Something was wrong.

The lurching way they moved made Lex pause and watch. It looked as if Taylor were having trouble staying on her feet, as if Eric were supporting part of her weight. The two of them staggered side by side.

Lex headed toward them, breaking into a run. "What's the matter?" he yelled.

The wind blasted his words away. He doubted that the two could even hear him. He ran closer. "What's the matter?"

"Get out of the way," Eric said irritably. "You're too little to carry her! Get some of the others, quick!"

"My foot hurts!" Taylor howled.

Then Lex saw a dribble of blood on the sand. Taylor's face was pale, almost greenish.

One fear hit Lex as hard as a fist in his stomach: *She's poisoned!*

Melissa faced the camera and, raising her voice above the whoosh of the wind, she began to talk:

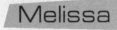

This morning, all our video diaries were stolen.

Eric told us that Lex had taken them, which I found hard to believe. But we had a trial, and it came out that Lex did take them so he could protect somebody's secret. He shouldn't have bothered. One way or the other, it was bound to come out, like all secrets do.

But anyway, we have the tapes back now, and I'm worried because—

She looked away from the lens, her attention jerked from the camera by someone yelling not far away. She reached out, her hand looming large in the camera lens as she stretched to press the off button.

Melissa jogged past the fire pit, over to the tents. Eric was supporting Taylor as they limped up the hill. Lex hovered behind them, his face frightened and uncertain. "What's wrong?" Melissa called.

"I can't carry her by myself! Little help here," Eric snapped, looking as if he had just about used the last of his energy supporting Taylor.

Daley was closer. She flew down the hillside and got on Taylor's right side. Between her and Eric, they helped Taylor up to the fire pit, to the big ice chest that had served as the judge's bench during their trial. Taylor pivoted on her right heel and sat down on the chest, wincing as she held her left foot off the ground.

"What happened?" Daley asked, looking from Taylor to Eric.

Melissa stopped a few feet away. Had Eric been goofing around the way he normally did? But Taylor looked okay, except for her face, wrenched by pain.

"I stepped on a rock or something in the water!" Taylor howled. "Oww, it hurts! Am I bleeding?"

"Hold still!" Daley knelt on the ground and managed to cup Taylor's left heel in the palm of her hand. "Taylor, don't squirm!"

Melissa saw Daley lean close, her pale blue eyes narrowed as she examined the sole of Taylor's foot. "No, it wasn't a rock," she said. "There's something still stuck in there."

"What!" Taylor shrieked. She flapped her arms and gave Eric a panic-stricken look. "Get it out! Get it out!" Then, to Melissa's surprise, she yanked her foot away from Daley's hold. "No, wait, that'll make it hurt more! Leave it in! Leave it in!"

"Can't do that," Lex said. "It could get infected, and then—"

"Infected?" Taylor screeched. "Eric, this is your fault!"

"Me?"

"Don't panic," Daley said. "Keep off your foot. I'll go and get the first-aid kit."

"Hurry!" Taylor ordered.

"How is it my fault?" Eric asked. "After I helped you up here and—"

"You distracted me when I was wading! If you hadn't been talking about Jackson and how you were gonna—"

"Shh, shh," Eric said hastily, waving his hands as though panicked.

Melissa narrowed her eyes in suspicion. How he was gonna—do what? Looking at Eric's guilty expression, she felt a flash of anger. "Eric! What is she talking about? *What* were you planning?"

"She's in pain!" Eric shot back. "Cut her some slack!" Lex started downhill, and Eric whirled to yell after him, "Where are you going, squirt?"

Without looking back, Lex said, "Plane. I need to take care of the radio."

Just then Daley hurried back up, holding onto the first-aid kit. With a worried frown, she said, "Taylor, maybe you'd better turn over onto your stomach. I can get a better look at your foot that way."

"This better not hurt," grumbled Taylor, but she twisted around and lay facedown on the top of the big ice chest. Her head and shoulders hung over the edge. She gripped the sides with her hands and bent her left knee, holding her foot up more or less parallel to the ground.

"Okay, I'm gonna rinse it with some of this," Daley said. "It's a painless antibiotic, so just hold still." She spritzed the ball of Taylor's foot and the base of her toes.

"Uhh—that's cold!" Taylor complained.

Melissa took a gauze pad from the kit and tore

it open. She handed it to Daley. "Thanks," Daley said as she gently swabbed the skin.

Melissa couldn't help flinching. The skin in the arch of Taylor's foot, just in front of her heel, showed an angry red welt, but the center was pale and white, with something dark showing under the surface. Melissa couldn't see very much blood—she'd had worse with scraped knees when she was just a little kid—but the wound *did* look swollen and painful.

Daley, holding Taylor's foot still, sucked in her breath and said, *"Eeyew!"*

Taylor looked back over her shoulder, her face a mixture of pain, anger, and fear. *"Eeyew?* Don't *eeyew* me! What is it?"

"I don't know," Daley confessed. She dabbed gently at the wound, and now Melissa saw just a trace of blood, just a tiny drop. The gauze pad, already wet from the antibiotic spray, picked up a pink tinge.

Daley leaned close and said thoughtfully, "This might be a piece of coral. Or it could be a stinger from some kind of sea animal."

"What!" Taylor yelped. *"Eeyew!"*

From behind Melissa came Nathan's voice: "Hey, guys, we've got a problem."

Taylor glared around at him. "Gee, you think?" She balled her hands into fists and beat on the sides of the ice chest she was lying on. *"Gaah!* I'm in agony here! Do something!"

"I'm not talking about you," Nathan said, and Melissa thought he sounded irritated. "Jackson's gone."

Daley turned around, still holding the gauze pad. She frowned in Nathan's direction. "Gone? What do you mean, *gone*? He probably just walked off to be alone after Eric—"

"No," Nathan said. "I mean he's cleared out, he's really gone. I just checked. All his gear is missing, and I can't find him anyplace."

Melissa felt a wave of shock. *First Abby, and now Jackson!* "But where would he go?"

Nathan shook his head helplessly. "I have no idea. But I can't really blame him after Eric's performance—"

"Hey," Eric said, "if you don't mind, I'm trying to give a little first aid here?"

Nathan gave him a quizzical look. Melissa could read Nathan's bewilderment. Eric was standing six feet away from the others and apparently not doing anything more important than taking up space. Nathan asked, "First aid?"

"In case you didn't notice," Taylor hissed between her clenched teeth, "I have been injured here. I'm not doing aerobics, you know!"

Thunder rolled again, making Melissa flinch. She saw Daley cast a worried glance up and then sweep her palm along her red hair, as if trying to smooth it down. "We've got to get Jackson back. Can you feel the electricity in the air?"

"No," Taylor snapped angrily, kicking her left foot back and forth, "but I can feel the harpoon in my foot!"

Nathan looked as antsy as Melissa felt. He shifted from foot to foot, and his eyes swept the threatening, dark horizon. "This storm is gonna be wicked," he said softly. "It's coming closer, too— it's sort of edging along in that direction, but the rain's a lot closer than it was twenty minutes ago." More thunder. "And I think the lightning's coming nearer, too."

Melissa's throat constricted. "And Jackson's out there in the wilderness somewhere, thinking we don't want him around. Abby and the others are out there, too. We have to get them to come back to shelter. We can't just—just ignore them."

"I don't know if we can find Abby," Daley said. "She's had too much of a start. But you're right about Jackson. We have to go look for him."

Taylor burst out, "Hel-lo! Injured!"

Daley shook her head at the others and said in a soothing way, "Okay, I'll try to get this thing out."

"Don't hurt me!" Taylor snapped. "Look, maybe if you, like, bandage it, and put some stuff on it, it will be okay. Okay?"

Daley gave Melissa a frustrated, helpless look. That made up Melissa's mind. "You do what you can for Taylor. I'm going to go look for Jackson."

"If she just wants me to put a bandage on it—"

"Yes!" Taylor said. "Yes, yes, yes! Bandage it, but put some of that stuff on it first. And don't hurt me!"

"Okay, and then I'm going to go with Melissa."

"Wait a minute," Nathan said. "She's got something stuck in her foot?"

"Yeah, coral or a stinger or something," Daley told him. "But she's afraid it will hurt if I try to take it out."

"It has to come out," Nathan said. "She's just asking for trouble if you leave it in. Daley, you deal with that, and I'll help Melissa look for Jackson. You'll have to stay here and help her."

"Somebody do something," Taylor said. "I'm getting uncomfortable here!"

"No biggie. *I'll* take care of Taylor," Eric volunteered.

"No," Nathan said, surprising Melissa with his angry tone. "You're coming with us."

"Go on," Daley said in a resigned voice. "I'll stay."

"Thank you," Taylor said sarcastically. "Now do something to stop it from hurting so much!"

"Wait a minute," Eric said, scowling at Nathan and Melissa. "Go with you two? No way! I'm not going anywhere!"

Melissa couldn't believe the bickering. She was ready to start, right now, right this second. "Forget Eric, Nathan. Come on," she urged.

"Eric is coming, too," Nathan insisted, his face set in an angry scowl.

"No, I'm not."

"Yeah, you are!"

Melissa thought the two boys were about to start pounding each other. Both looked furious. Then Nathan moved forward suddenly, startling Eric so that he stepped back—but he couldn't go far because of a tree behind him. In the blink of an eye, Nathan stood totally in Eric's face. His voice dropped to an intense, commanding growl: "I'll say this once, and I'll say it as clear as I can. It's your fault Jackson is out there, Eric. And you're going to help us find him and bring him back here. Got it?"

Melissa hesitated only for a moment. Then she stepped forward to stand right beside Nathan. "He's right," she said.

Eric tried crossing his arms again, but they didn't want to stay crossed, and when he hooked his thumbs in the pockets of his shorts, he looked defensive and sullen. "Fine," he said at last. "Hey, whatever. But when it starts to rain, I'm gone." He sidled toward a chair and picked up a pair of beach shoes, kicking off his sandals as he did.

"Come on, let's get started." Nathan gestured toward the waiting jungle. "After you, Eric."

Melissa fell in beside Nathan as they walked away from camp. Nathan whispered to her, "Let's keep him in front, where we can watch him."

Though she had supported Nathan, Melissa was secretly wondering whether even taking Eric was a good idea.

But then, she wasn't in charge.

Lex had climbed back up and had reattached the antenna. Somehow, he felt an urgency to make one more attempt before the storm really hit. Because he had a very bad feeling about this storm.

A storm had put them here in the first place, a great sprawling monster of a squall that spread out so far, Captain Russell had not been able to fly around it. It had speared their starboard engines with a spiked trident of lightning, had burst the engines into flame, and had sent the Heron pancaking down, skipping on the lagoon, plowing up into the beach.

If the approaching storm were as bad as the first one—

Lex checked his watch. Time to try again. Carefully, he hauled the radio inside the plane. Sitting there in the open doorway, his legs dangling, he turned the power on and looked at the readouts. Everything *looked* okay. He keyed the mike and varied his distress call: "Mayday, Mayday."

Lex licked his lips and repeated, "Mayday,

Mayday. This is Two-niner Delta William November. This is DeHavilland Heron Two-niner Delta William November. We are alive, but we need help."

Thunder crashed, making him wince. When it had died away, he repeated the call once more, then listened.

Static. It scratched inside the speakers.

Nothing but static.

THIRTEEN

They had plunged into the forest and into deep gloom. The clouds overhead shut off part of the sun. The dense emerald-colored canopy of foliage cut off even more. To Nathan the light had a surreal quality, as if they were in an immense aquarium, as if the water were letting in just a green-tinged, sickly glimmer.

At least the wind wasn't as much of a problem here. They could hear it thrashing in the tops of the trees, but what broke through the thick vegetation was just enough to stir the air a little. Beside Nathan, Melissa paused and cupped her hands at the sides of her mouth. "Jackson!" she bellowed. "Jack . . . son! Hello!"

Eric, still a few steps ahead, didn't stop, slow, or even look around. "This is stupid. He could be anywhere."

Nathan heard more thunder from up above. The trees here weren't all that big, more like healthy saplings than full-grown jungle giants. In fact, most of them were only about as thick as a fire hose. Their progress was going to get a lot tougher as they reached the real woods. The jungle would grow a lot denser before it thinned out again.

Did they have a chance of finding Jackson? Nathan didn't know. Right here, in this stretch, they could see only a couple of dozen yards ahead. When the real jungle began, when the big trees grew so thick that the undergrowth was choked off, it would be darker, harder to see than here, even. And sound wouldn't carry as far, so calling Jackson would be even—

Something crept over his neck, and he slapped at an insect. He felt it crush into a wet ball and flicked it off his hand.

"We're way past the banana trees," Melissa said. "Up ahead are the heavy woods, and then the hills."

"Yeah," Nathan said. "I know."

"So how far do we go?"

"As far as it takes."

Melissa was quiet for a long moment, and then she said, "Maybe he's going to try to catch up with Abby."

Could be. Nathan had almost forgotten Abby, after all that had happened today. But it just might be possible that Jackson thought he'd help her track down Captain Russell, Ian, and Jory. The trouble was, they had no idea what path Abby might have taken. Their group had explored some way into the jungle, and Nathan had a hunch that Jackson would follow trails he knew. But Abby could be anywhere, in any direction.

Up ahead, Eric had stopped. Nathan caught up and prodded him in the back. "Keep moving," he said.

"But this is stupid!"

"Just—just keep going."

It wasn't very much of a plan, but Nathan had to admit he didn't set out with a plan.

Just the deep conviction that somehow they had to find Jackson.

Because, though it was a little hard for Nathan to admit it, Jackson was a better leader than he could be. Jackson had something, a kind of quiet authority. He was the glue that held them all together. Without him, they wouldn't stand a chance of surviving.

So they had to find Jackson, they just *had* to.

Not just for his sake.

For theirs.

Daley had laid out everything in the kit. She hesitated, because she knew that what she had to do would hurt Taylor. And she knew that Taylor would let her know about it. Well, maybe she wouldn't kick.

Although Daley couldn't count on that.

"What is it?" Taylor whimpered.

"I won't know until I get it out," Daley said. And maybe not even then. It wasn't as though she were a nurse or anything.

Next to the ice chest, a pair of stainless-steel medical forceps, like extra-large tweezers, stood propped up in a cup. Daley had poured in an inch of alcohol.

How long did it take alcohol to sterilize medical instruments? Lex might know, but Lex had gone off somewhere.

The radio. Of course. Lex had a schedule: Listen and call four times every single day. That's where he would be.

"What do you *think* it is?" Taylor asked.

"I couldn't guess," Daley admitted. "I don't know what's in the ocean around here. It might be a sea urchin—"

"A sea what?"

"Sea urchin. It looks kind of like an underwater porcupine."

"Eeyew!"

"Or it might even be something like a stingray. I can't tell."

"It hurts." Taylor put her head down, then asked in a softer voice, "Stingrays aren't, like, poisonous, though, right?"

"Some are."

Taylor sprang up and spun in midair, coming down to sit on the chest, her eyes round and popping. "What! Poisonous? No! Wait, are you serious?"

Daley bent down and picked up the cup. She took the forceps out and shook the alcohol off. "Just turn over and relax. We have to get this out."

Taylor screwed her face up, staring at the forceps. She whimpered, and Daley came close to feeling sorry for her.

"Turn back over," she said gently. "I'll be as quick as I can, and I'll try not to hurt you."

"Okay," Taylor said in a miserable voice. She carefully turned over again and lay along the top of the ice chest. She raised her trembling foot.

Daley took a deep breath and hoped she knew what she was doing.

Halfway up a hillside, in a thicket of bamboo, a louder crash of thunder caught the searchers. The noise here was worse than ever, the bamboo clattering and rattling all around them. It was *intense*.

Not like applause, no sir, not at all. More like the theater's about to be blown away in a hurricane or a tornado. Well, folks, it's been fun, but that's our show for tonight.

Eric threw his hands up. "That's it. I'm outta here," he announced, turning to head back.

Nathan stepped to head him off. "Eric—"

Eric caught a note of desperation, a hint of fear, in Nathan's voice. So the big man wasn't so big after all. And, hey, face it, if it came down to a struggle, Melissa sure wasn't gonna help, was she?

No, not at all, thank you very much. Well, if Nathan wanted to play this little scene, he could play it with Melissa. Eric had enough sense to be elsewhere.

Eric sidestepped Nathan and, on the downhill side, said, "Hey, if you want to get stuck out here in the middle of a lightning storm looking for some lowlife who doesn't even like us, that's fine. Your choice." He watched warily. Had he read Nathan right? It was one thing to be all brave and overbearing back in camp, but up here on the hill, half a mile or more past the point any of them had been so far, it was different, wasn't it? Wasn't quite the same with the lightning forking and the wind slapping the bamboo around.

"Listen, Eric," Nathan said. "Abby and the others may be out in this, hurt or sick. And I know we *need* Jackson. We have to stand together, or else—"

"You're scaring Melissa," Eric said.

"I'm not scared," Melissa countered at once, though she *looked* terrified.

Eric tilted his hat back. He had brought a

jacket, just in case of rain, and now he pulled it on. "Okay, have it your way. You two do whatever you want. Look for Jackson. Have a picnic. Have a freakin' Senior Prom if you want. But me, I'm going back."

He turned and headed back downhill. Behind him, he heard Melissa say to Nathan, "No, don't go after him. It's okay. We'll be better off without him."

Yes!

Eric chuckled to himself. Melissa was such a wimp. Okay, so he could come on a little strong now and then, and sometimes, tell the truth, it bothered him when people didn't seem to like him, when they made cracks like "We'll be better off without him." But it was one thing to be bothered, another to be caught in a hurricane. *And anyway,* Eric thought, *I'll sure be better off without* them!

Better off without Jackson, too.

"Jackson!" It was Nathan yelling this time, already a good way behind Eric. He broke into a trot, easier going downhill than trudging up the slope. With luck, he'd be back in camp in a few minutes. Maybe the rain would hold off at least that long.

Let Nathan and Melissa get soaked. Serve them right. Serve them right if the lightning—

Well, hey, maybe not.

No sense in going *too* far.

Sitting in the open doorway of the plane, Lex had tried all the frequencies. He started around the dial again. Something in the air told him it was urgent, that he didn't have much time. If the storm made the slightest turn, this might be their last chance to use the radio for days.

He repeated his distress call and listened again to the maddening scratch of static. What was he doing *wrong*? Maybe his idea about getting the antenna higher might be the secret. Maybe they could rig some kind of tower. Cut down the tallest bamboo they could find, lash it together, maybe make a tower about thirty feet tall, and put the antenna—

Wait a minute. Jackson had the knife.

Lex started to tune the radio to the next frequency when he heard his own name, shouted over the boom of surf and the rush of the wind. He turned his head, unsure of whether he had just imagined his sister's voice, but then he saw her, up toward the tents, beckoning to him and yelling for him. He leaped down, wondering if something else had happened.

"What is it?" he puffed as he drew near Daley.

"Come on," she said. "I've got to try to take a stinger or something out of Taylor's foot, and

I need help. Every time I touch her, she says it hurts, and she pulls away from me."

"What do you expect me to do?"

"I don't know!" Lex jumped in surprise at how angry she sounded. Daley put a hand up to her mouth. "I—don't know. But the others are off hunting Jackson, and I don't have anyone to—"

"I'll do what I can," Lex promised.

"Come on." Daley led him to the spot where Taylor waited.

Taylor seemed to be in great discomfort. "Hurry," she complained.

"Well, if you wouldn't jerk your foot every time I touched it—"

"Well, if you wouldn't hurt me—"

"Wait a minute," Lex said. He rummaged in a backpack and found a blue bandanna. He quickly folded it up into a four-inch pad and handed it to Taylor. "Here," he said. "Bite it."

Taylor's face turned scarlet. "What! You little—"

"No!" Lex yelled. "Bite this when your foot starts to hurt. That'll help distract you from the pain."

Taylor gave him an incredulous look.

"Come on," Lex wheedled. "Haven't you ever seen any adventure movies, where the wounded guy bites on a bullet?"

"Bites on a—"

"Just try it."

Taylor made a face at the roll of bandage. "If this doesn't work—"

"It'll work. Trust me."

Taylor put the bandanna between her teeth and grunted.

Daley began to work on her foot with the medical forceps, and immediately Taylor twitched, jerking her foot away. "*Mmff!* It hurts!" she yelled, her words muffled by the cloth in her mouth.

"Ugh, I need three hands!" Daley gasped. "Lex, come here. I need you to help."

Lex went around and, at Daley's direction, he grasped Taylor's ankle. "Now try to hold that nice and steady while—"

Lex whipped his head around, looking down toward the plane. "*Shh!*"

"What?"

"I thought I heard—" He listened, but all he could really hear was the wind. "Nothing, I guess," he said. "Okay. I'm ready."

The radio crackled with static. Then, faintly, a voice, sounding faraway and thin, came over the speaker:

"*Did not copy your Mayday transmission. Please identify.*"

Scratch . . . scratch . . .

Just static.

Then again:

"Person sending the Two-niner Mayday call, please respond. Did not fully copy you. Please identify, Two-niner. Repeat, Two-niner, did not copy you. Please identify . . ."

No one heard.

No one was close enough to hear.

FOURTEEN

They had toiled up to the top of a hill and for the moment stood in a clearing. Behind them lay a tossing green landscape, wind-fingered and heaving like a sea of leaves. Melissa could still hear the clatter of the bamboo thicket, now far behind them. Ahead was a dark green wall of jungle, and beyond that reared the shoulders of a volcanic mountain, its top lost in the low, surging mass of cloud.

Melissa held her canvas hat in place and turned 360 degrees. No sign of Jackson. No sign of Eric, for that matter. She didn't like this at all.

Nathan yelled for Jackson again, but the wind seemed to muffle the hoarse sound of his voice.

Something stung Melissa's hand, and she looked at it, saw a wet splash. "Uh-oh."

"What?" Nathan barked, edgy, tense.

Melissa held her hand out. "Rain."

Nathan glanced up at the sky and then, nervously, muttered, "Maybe we should head back. We don't want to be caught out here."

Neither would Jackson, Melissa thought. She heard the plop as three or four more fat raindrops smashed into the rocky top of the hill. The jungle wasn't too far ahead. Surely it would offer some protection. She made up her mind and started forward, yelling, "Jack-son!"

Loose rock skittered under her feet, and she windmilled her arms to get her balance back. Half a dozen steps, half running, half falling, and then she was okay again, heading down into a valley. On the far side the real woods started, dark and threatening.

She had gone a dozen more steps when Nathan's voice stopped her. "Mel!"

She turned to look back. Nathan still stood up on the crest of the hill, his hair whipping in the wind. "What?" she asked.

He held out a hand as if offering to help her climb back up. "We really don't want to get caught out here in a storm."

"But Jackson—"

"He'd say it would be better for just one to be out than three of us. Come on. Time to turn back. We'll look when this passes over."

Melissa stood in indecision. The thunder was constant now, a surrounding growl and grumble.

More raindrops, hard ones, struck her.

Nathan was right, though. Jackson was always practical. Better for one to be lost in the storm than three.

Or four.

Where was Eric?

Or five. "Do you think Abby's safe?" Melissa asked apprehensively.

"I hope so," Nathan said. "I hope everyone's somewhere safe. We'd better get back."

"Okay," Melissa said, giving in. She labored back up to the top of the hill and headed back the way they had come. Behind her, she heard Nathan following.

Now it was worse. The rain was in their faces, hitting so hard that it stung.

But it wasn't going to get better. Not any time soon.

Rain. Oh, great. Oh, wonderful. This is just what I needed, this puts the cherry on top of the whole lousy day. Thank you very much.

Eric glared up at the ragged underbelly of the sky. "Thank you *very* much," he yelled.

The sky answered by throwing a blast of stinging rain right in his upturned face. He ducked away and wiped his eyes. He hurried downhill, skidding and slipping on the wet grass.

What had happened to the freaking bamboo? He was sure they'd passed through a wide stand of it, across spongy, oozing ground. But now he was in a thicket of ferny-looking stuff, frilly brush that grew higher than his head and gave, like, *zero* protection from the rain and wind. In fact, he wanted to get *out* of this as soon as he could, because it wasn't any fun to have a frond of fern slap you—*ouch!*—right in the open eyes.

Maybe if he sort of climbed up sideways he could get to a clearing and see where he was. He hunched along, hood pulled up but useless as the wind found ways of pouring cold rain down his neck. He could feel his straw hat getting soggy.

He emerged onto a sort of shelf, bare dark-gray volcanic rock. Trees loomed ahead of him, taller than the ones he remembered coming through on the way out. And where was the bamboo?

"Oh, man," Eric muttered in disgust. "I am *not* believing this."

Hold on, though. You're on an island, right? Right. Well, an island is surrounded by the ocean, right? Right. And the ocean is at sea level, see? Sí. So, see, find the sea. All you have to do is go downhill. Get to the beach, and you can find your way back to the plane.

Good, solid reasoning. Nathan couldn't have done better. Hey, fugitive-on-the-run-from-the-law Jackson couldn't have done better.

Downhill, that was the ticket.

To the ocean.

Eric picked a direction, hunched his shoulders, and jogged on.

The rain had not reached the camp, but now Daley could hear it not far away, hissing down into the undergrowth up the hillside. Lex stood beside her, his small hands holding Taylor's ankle. He was straining to hold her foot still, his top teeth biting into his lower lip.

Daley had already tried twice to get the forceps to clamp onto the little chunk of—whatever—that showed in Taylor's foot. But every time she touched the skin—and she couldn't *help* touching the skin—Taylor screeched and kicked. Now she was jerking her foot in *anticipation* of the forceps.

"Taylor, just hold still!" Daley snapped.

"Yeah," Lex grunted. "Stop squirming!"

Taylor made fists and pounded the sides of the ice chest she lay on. "I can't help it!" she screamed. "It hurts, it hurts, it hurts!"

"The more you fight, the longer it's going to take," warned Daley. "I'll *try* not to hurt you, but you're going to have to hold still. Lex, steady her foot."

Lex's fingers paled as he tightened his grip. He braced Taylor's toes against his chest, stopping her twitching and jerking.

"Oww! Stop *pinching!"* Taylor moaned. Daley saw her snake her hand back and grab Lex's bare leg just under the hem of his shorts. She gave his skin a vicious squeeze, making him squirm.

"Oww!" Lex roared in pain and anger. *"You* stop pinching!"

Daley took a deep breath. This was like being on a kindergarten playground, the one big kid trying to break up a fight between two little brats who didn't like each other very much. But at the moment, Lex had Taylor's foot immobilized. With her left fingers, Daley pressed the sole of Taylor's foot, and she saw the dark gleam of something showing through a rip in the skin.

"Hang on!" she yelled. She brought the forceps up, then carefully pressed the jaws down, around the dark shape.

"A little bit more . . . hold her foot still, Lex, I've almost got it—"

A high-pitched, keening whine burst from Taylor. "Oww! *Owww!* Stop!"

Daley felt a throb of misgiving. Taylor was really hurting, and she wasn't a girl who was used to hurting. But she could feel the grate of something through the metal of the forceps. She almost had it. Blood was oozing now, making the thing slippery. She didn't want the forceps to slip—got it, got it—

"Aahhh!" Taylor shuddered, but Daley could tell she was making a real effort not to kick

anymore. Taylor gasped and then sobbed, "It hurts, Daley! It's getting worse! It really hurts! Oh, don't do any more, please. Don't . . . don't . . ."

Daley was so focused on what she was doing she didn't even feel sick. She pulled the forceps slowly away, and with them came *something* an inch long, dark brownish-red, thin, and wickedly sharp. Blood dripped from the open wound it left behind, and strings of, *ugh*, some slimy stuff oozed off the tip of the stinger, if that was what it was.

Taylor was still crying and writhing. "Daley, I can't take it, stop, please just stop!"

With a weary feeling of triumph, Daley moved around and held up the stinger-looking object in front of Taylor's face. "Hey. Take a look."

"Look at what? I can't stand the pain, Daley, you're gonna make me—" Taylor's voice trailed off as she opened her eyes and focused on the ugly spike clamped in Daley's forceps. "Oh . . . oh, it's out?"

"Like it was never there," Daley said. She dropped the stinger into the cup with the alcohol—Nathan would want to take a look at it, and maybe he'd even know what it was—and then put a gob of antibiotic on the wound. She covered that with a square bandage. "The antibiotic goo it has a pain reliever in it, too, so you should feel better soon."

"What was it?" Taylor asked weakly as Lex finally released her ankle.

"I don't know," Daley said, picking up the cup

and staring down at the ugly spike she had pulled out of Taylor's foot. "But whatever it is, it's big."

"You know what?" Taylor asked in a contrite, little-girl voice.

"What?"

"I'm gonna faint." Her head dropped down, and she went limp.

Lex threw up his hands. "Oh, great. *Now* she's not moving!"

Daley started to laugh, although part of her, for some reason, felt like crying instead.

Come on, come on, it's simple—downhill, to the beach—

Eric was out of breath. And rapidly getting soaked from the drumming rain. Down the hill, sure, but once you got to the bottom of *this* hill, the problem was that ahead was *another* hill, and nothing looked familiar at all!

On the side of the hill that lay ahead—and was it shorter or taller than the one he had just left? Visibility was so poor that he couldn't tell. Anyway, on the side of *that* hill, trees grew thick. They promised shelter.

Lightning sizzled, and thunder slammed the ground like the fist of an angry giant.

Wasn't there something about not going under a tree in a thunderstorm?

Eric picked a direction and ran.

Panic ran with him, nipping at his heels like an angry dog.

The echoes of the thunder bounced back from the distant mountains.

Lost, the thunder seemed to growl.

Lost, lost, lost.

FIFTEEN

Lex felt the first drops of rain on his bare arm. "Hurry," he told his sister.

The three of them, Taylor, Daley, and Lex, sat huddled under the fire pit canopy. The wind was making it flap and snap overhead. If the rain really turned loose, the canopy wouldn't give them any protection. Daley was winding gauze around Taylor's instep, having decided that the bandage might come loose unless something else held it down. "You can put a sock over that," she said. "That'll help pad it."

Taylor looked positively green. She had recovered from her faint and had immediately thrown up, to Lex's disgust. "Poison?" she asked in a small voice.

"Look, I don't know what the thing was," Daley said. "Probably not."

"You said stingrays are poisonous!"

"Actually," Lex said, "most rays are harmless. And even the dangerous ones will get out of your way if you shuffle your feet when you're in the water. They're like snakes—"

"*Snakes?*" Taylor's eyes were wild. "It wasn't a snake, was it? Some kind of sea snake or something—"

"It wasn't a snake," Daley said. "I don't know what that thing is, but I know for sure it isn't a snake fang."

Taylor whimpered, tears running down her cheeks. "You said it would feel better."

"Does it hurt as much?"

Taylor looked as though she were in agony. "I can't tell! I can't remember how much it hurt before! But if it was poisonous, am I gonna, like, swell up and die?"

Lex heard Daley mutter under her breath, "Hopefully."

Taylor jerked her foot. Fortunately, Daley had just finished taping down the end of the gauze. "What? What?"

Daley gave her a reassuring smile and a little pat on the shoulder. "I said you're gonna be fine."

"Don't worry," Lex said. "Most venoms aren't necessarily fatal."

"Necessarily?"

"You have to stay calm, keep your foot elevated—"

"What do you mean?" Taylor demanded. She turned to Daley. "What does he mean, elevated?"

"Lie down, prop your foot up, and don't move too much," Daley translated. "Hey, is that—"

Lex jumped up. Nathan and Melissa had just emerged from the trail to the banana trees. Was Jackson with them?

No.

Nathan saw them, and he and Melissa came hurrying over, bending against the wind and the fitful spatters of rain. Taylor was whimpering and whining now like a two-year-old, big tears spilling from her eyes and dripping from her chin. Even her nose was running.

As Nathan and Melissa ducked under the scant cover of the canopy, Taylor burst out in a petulant complaint: "You left me alone with her! It was horrible! She—she was like some kind of medieval witch doctor!"

Lex rolled his eyes and saw Nathan suppress a smile. Lex said, "There is no such thing as a medieval witch doctor. Witch doctors are—"

They weren't listening to him again. Daley said anxiously, "What happened? No Jackson?"

Nathan shook his head. He looked wet, soaked in fact, as if the rain that had held off here had already hit inland. "We didn't have any luck," he said. "The storm started moving in, so we came back. I guess Abby hasn't showed up, huh?"

"No," Daley said. "I hope she and the others are somewhere safe."

Melissa asked, "Where's Eric?"

Daley blinked at her. "Huh? What do you mean? Eric went with you guys!"

Nathan turned to stare up the hill, toward the jungle. "Eric started back alone an hour ago or more. He should be here already."

Lex said, "He hasn't turned up."

"Oh, man," Taylor said in a voice that was no longer frightened. Now it just sounded ticked off.

But Lex didn't feel anger.

He felt a dull ache of dread. If they separated, if they broke up, if they couldn't rely on each other—

"Here comes the rain," Melissa yelled. "We'd better get into the tent!"

It came down the hill in a gray curtain, a hissing wall of rain. They raced it, diving into the girls' tent just in time. Lex closed the flap as the rain snapped into the canvas and then settled into a steady drumming.

"Eric and Jackson are out in *this*?" Taylor wailed.

The light in the tent, already dimmed, failed and faded. Lex realized that it was late afternoon, but the darkness of the storm was more intense than that.

This was going to be a bad one.

It couldn't get much worse, man.

Eric was scared to be out in the open, where white-hot lightning tore open the sky just *inches*— well, it *felt* like inches—over his head. And he was scared to be in the forest, where it was *dark*, man, dark as the inside of a vampire-bat cave, and the thunder made the trees quiver, and the blasts of wind ripped the canopy apart and spilled rivers of rain down over his head and shoulders.

He made a dash, found himself floundering in an ankle-high torrent of runoff that hadn't been there a second ago, skidded, crashed to the ground, and rolled, mud stinging his eyes, filling his mouth. He pushed himself up, bruised and dazed, spitting and coughing. The jungle. He plunged beneath the trees, ran stumbling for fifty or sixty feet, caught his toe on a root, went flat on his stomach again—

Oh, man, oh, man.

It *was* worse.

"I'm scared, Dad," he groaned. "What do I do now?"

But for once his dad had no answers to offer him. Not even in his imagination.

Melissa huddled miserably in the tent. It was hard to talk above the hammering of the rain and the constant roar of thunder. Her heart was in her throat, and she felt as though the air she gasped in had no oxygen in it, as if it were lifeless, stale, and did her no good. "Now they're both lost out there," she mumbled.

"Eric and Jackson aren't the only ones," Lex said. When Melissa looked at him, he said, "Don't forget Abby and the others."

"We have to do something," Melissa said.

Daley put her hand on Melissa's arm. "What should we do?" Melissa had no answer for that, and Daley added, in a kind voice, "What can we do?"

In the gloom, Nathan's eyes looked huge. He sat huddled up and said, "We wait."

The rain squall blew over, and Nathan cautiously opened the tent flap. It was nearly as dark outside as in. "Is it clearing up?" Melissa asked.

"No. There's more coming. It's really dark out over the lagoon." Nathan suddenly stiffened. "What's that?"

"What?" Melissa craned to look past him. "I don't see any—"

"No, it's a sound. Listen."

Melissa held her breath. In the intervals between gusts of wind, peals of thunder, *was* there another sound? She wasn't sure at first, and then she heard it, a crackling, odd, electrical noise. "I hear something," she said.

"Me, too," Daley added. "It's some kind of . . . static from the storm."

"Yeah, I think so, too," Nathan said. "But where is it coming from?"

"I've read about Saint Elmo's fire," Lex said. "That's a kind of electrical display you get at sea. It's called a corona discharge—"

Melissa cut him off. "*Shh.* There it is again."

Lex stopped talking.

In the moment of silence, Melissa caught something very clearly: it was the word "copy," in a scratchy, staticky voice.

She leaped to her feet, her heart feeling as if it were about to explode with excitement. "Did you hear that?"

Lex jumped up at the same instant, wild hope in his face. "It's the radio!"

He tore off, with Melissa right behind him. The radio! They were saved!

SIXTEEN

The gusting wind buffeted the plane, making it rock back and forth, as if it were about to rev up and take off. Rain lashed in from the sea, drumming on the wings and the fuselage. A stronger blast made the antenna whip back and forth, loosening the ties that bound it to the bamboo pole, whipping the bamboo itself back and forth.

Inside the plane, the forgotten radio crackled and buzzed. A different sound came through, not static, but the deep background roar of jet engines. Then through the speakers a man's voice broke out, so loud and clear he might have been just a few miles away.

"Did not copy. Please repeat, Two-niner. I say again, we could not copy your last transmission. Identify—"

Wind peppered with hail blasted in, an engulfing, howling chaos. The antenna caught it, twisted in its bindings. With a damp *crack!* the bamboo pole parted, and the antenna broke free and sailed off the roof of the plane. The connecting wires jerked it back, and it toppled onto the wing, then fell to the sand behind the wing.

The speakers scratched random sound. No voice now.

Just the scratching noise of static.

Daley led the charge down to the beach, through a new and fiercer rain squall. It came sweeping in from the lagoon, heavy and blinding, and in only three steps the horizontal rain had soaked her to the skin. Running just behind her, Lex was a close second, his short legs pumping. Behind them hurried Melissa, and last of all, Nathan helped Taylor stumble on through the rain.

Daley half-turned, her eyes assaulted by the downpour. "Ouch!" Round chips of opaque white ice the size of dimes smacked into her, stinging and sharp. She could hear it rattling on the airplane's wings.

"What's that?" Taylor shrieked. "Is that *snow*?"

"Hail!" Lex barked over his shoulder.

"Don't you use that kind of language—"

"It's hail!" Lex repeated. "Ice! You get it in bad thunderstorms!"

They reached the plane and found a scant shelter in the lee of the fuselage. Daley heard the metallic *spang!* sounds of hail bouncing off the wings. The whole plane seemed to tremble in the wind, as if, earthbound though it was, it yearned to take off. Lex shoved past her and scrambled up onto the wing, then swung into the open doorway. On hands and knees, he lunged forward, grabbed the mike and keyed it. "Is somebody there? Mayday!"

Nathan forced Taylor to lean against the plane and looked up at Lex. He yelled, "What is it?"

Behind Daley, Melissa, her voice sharp with hope, asked, "Is it a plane?"

And almost at the same moment, Taylor asked, "Are we rescued?"

Lex made impatient shushing gestures, slashing his hand down and back, and then he fiddled with the dials of the radio. He held the mike to his mouth again and said, "Mayday, Mayday. This is the wreck of the DeHavilland Heron Two-niner Delta William November. Do you read me?"

Daley listened harder than she had ever listened in her life, straining forward, rising on her tiptoes. She could even hear the blood pounding in her own arteries and veins.

But the radio speaker was silent except for its maddening, scratchy static.

Lex bent over and spoke again, louder, with urgency, as if he could force someone to hear him through sheer effort: "Mayday, Mayday. Flight Two-niner Delta William November is down. We are alive. Repeat: We are alive. Mayday. Does anyone read me? Over."

Nothing.

Daley hugged herself and asked Nathan, "Would a search plane be out in this storm?"

Before Nathan could answer, Lex cut in impatiently: "Doesn't have to be someone *looking* for us. It could be any plane that's flying nearby, a regular airliner or an Air Force plane or something." He was twiddling the radio dials again, but nothing seemed to help. Daley saw his face clench in frustration.

Taylor made an impatient noise. "Lex! Talk to *them,* not us! Go on, tell them we're here and we need to be rescued!"

"I'm doing my best!" Lex yelled back, his face red in the quickly fading light.

Daley felt sorry for him. Why couldn't the passing plane have called this morning, when things were dry? "You can do it, Lex," she said encouragingly.

"Oh, please let them hear!" Melissa sobbed. It was a prayer, Daley realized. "Please, oh, please!"

Lex was trying the microphone again, his tense voice rising as he made the call. "Mayday. Mayday. This is flight Two-niner Delta William November. We have crashed. We are in distress. Please respond. Over."

Melissa leaned against Daley. Her voice was anguished: "What's wrong? Why can't we hear them anymore?"

"I don't know!" Lex looked tormented.

"Try again!" Taylor wailed.

"Come on, come on," Nathan chanted.

"Keep trying," Daley said. "Try everything you know."

"Mayday," Lex repeated into the microphone. Under his breath, he muttered, "Come on, somebody, come on. You have to hear me. You've *got* to!"

Eric caught his foot and fell, exhausted. He was sopping wet, muddy, scratched, bruised, banged up, and still completely lost. Night was coming on fast. He saw a shadowy bulk ahead, forced himself to his feet, and stumbled on.

Tree, a big one. Giant of the forest.

Except some *past* storm had knocked this one over. The tree's roots had ripped free of the earth and the trunk had toppled, but other trees had caught it. It never quite reached the ground.

Now the vast trunk lay at a shallow angle. Off to one side, the roots had torn free. Far off to the other side, the top branches had caught, tangled, and now supported the dead trunk eight or ten feet from the ground.

Underneath the trunk the ground was dry. Relatively dry.

Okay, okay, it was humid, soggy, saturated, mucky, muddy, boggy, swampy, drenched, dripping, sodden.

Ladies and gentlemen, let us face it. It's wet.

But, yes, *wet* was a relative term and *dry* was equally relative, and so, relatively speaking, the space that was mostly wet was relatively dry. As compared to Eric, for instance.

You could wring Eric out and produce enough water to satisfy the thirst of a herd of camels. Good thing the twilight was fairly warm, or he'd be shivering in his shoes.

Come to think of it, he *was* shivering. It really wasn't all that warm.

Not when you were as wet as Eric, and not when the wind was blowing as hard as it was.

He wasn't just relatively wet, either. In fact, he was absolutely *soaked*.

"Oh, man," Eric moaned, huddling himself into as small a ball as possible beneath the marginal shelter of the fallen tree trunk. "I don't wanna die out here."

Not much of a punch line, fella.

Not much of a joke, to tell you the truth.

Lightning struck a tree not very far away, hit it with a sound like dynamite exploding, and the rain seemed to be encouraged by the noise and sheeted down even heavier than before.

Eric shoved himself back until he had to bend his head forward. If it was raining this hard up in the mountains, if the rain was pouring down in buckets way up there, where the shoulders of the mountains looked like bare rock with nothing to soak up the deluge, then it was going to run right off in a flood. If he stayed here, would he be in the path of a wall of water? He tried to imagine it, brown water frothing and foaming into the forest, uprooting trees, sweeping everything away.

He needed to reach higher ground, but at the moment his legs wouldn't carry him.

Maybe the rain would let up. Maybe if he rested—

"I don't wanna die out here," he said again, shivering in the growing darkness, in the unending rain.

Lex was feeling increasingly upset. He had tried all the frequencies and now was starting over again, at the old original one that—maybe—someone had responded to. "Mayday," he croaked, his voice strained from tension. "Mayday.

To all receivers: Flight Two-niner Delta William November has crashed. We are the survivors of the crash. We are all alive and need help as soon as possible. We—"

With an almighty boom, lightning slammed into the hillside maybe a mile away. Lex dropped the microphone, nearly convulsing.

"What's wrong?" Daley's concerned voice cut in as the thunder died down. "Lex, answer me! Are you okay?"

Lex nodded, then realized that Daley couldn't see him. Night had fallen. "Yeah," he said. "Noise just scared me, that's all. But if I'm holding the microphone and lightning strikes the antenna— well, no more Lex."

"What?" said Taylor. Lex had had just about enough of Taylor. His chest still ached where she had kicked him while Daley was trying to help her. Now Taylor sounded childish and angry, as if she were scolding him: "Don't be a wuss, Lex! How bad could it be?"

"I could get fried!" Lex shouted back at her.

"No, you couldn't! I've listened to the radio when it was raining lots of times, and—"

"Fine!" Lex yelled. "Okay, then you come up here and do it."

"Go ahead," Daley said, her tone mocking. "Lex can show you how."

To Lex's surprise, after a moment of hesitation, Taylor limped forward. "Somebody help me climb up," she said.

Nathan gave her a boost onto the wing. "*Eeyew,* it's slippery!" Taylor complained, her knees skidding on the wet metal. But she crept up the wing on all fours and then hoisted herself through the open doorway.

"Move aside," Daley said from a perch on the wing behind her. "Let us in out of the storm."

They all scrambled inside, the whole soaked pack of them, clustering around the radio. "What do I do?" Taylor asked.

"I'll do it," Lex said with a sigh.

But Taylor had picked up the microphone. "Just tell me what to do! Anything is better than being stuck out here."

"Push the button on the side when you talk, let it go when you finish and want to listen," Lex told her.

Taylor swept her wet hair back out of her face and said, "Hello? Hello? This is Taylor Hagan. I'm the one you've been looking for. Get me out of here!"

The plane shuddered in the wind, and Lex heard a scratching, metallic noise—not static, but something brushing against the metal skin of the plane outside. There were no bushes close— what could that be? He turned and scrambled over to look out a starboard window. In the flicker and glare of lightning, he could just make out something trailing down from the roof of the plane—a loose wire—

"Hello?" Taylor was still speaking into the

mike. "Hel-lo? Taylor Hagan here! Come on, don't make me—"

Realization slammed into Lex just as he felt someone's hand on his shoulder. Nathan. Nathan peered out the window next to him. *"Hey!"*

Taylor shrieked and threw the mike away from her. It clonked against Lex's leg as she screamed, *"Aah!* What happened? What, Nathan? Am I okay?"

"Not you—the antenna!" Nathan yelled. "It's blown off, I can see the wire!" He dived out the door. A second later, Lex saw him reappear on the port side of the plane. Nathan snatched up the antenna assembly—it looked like a stubby spear that a boomerang had partly penetrated—and waved it. He unhooked the wires and vanished again, ducking to the port side, where the open door was.

Lex stepped out of the door and leaped down onto the sand just as Nathan reappeared, brandishing the antenna high over his head, as if it were a trophy he'd just won. Lex dived for him. "Nathan! No!" He swatted at Nathan's arm, and Nathan, more surprised than anything, lost his hold, dropping the antenna.

Nathan stepped back, holding off Lex, hands on the smaller boy's shoulders. "What, are you crazy? Lex, we've got to get it back up!"

"Not now!" Lex flinched as lightning crackled overhead. "And don't hold it up in the air like that! That thing's like a lightning rod!"

Nathan's expression was hard to read in the flickering reflections of lightning. He looked— baffled, furious, scared. "What? You must be kidding me!" One of his hands swept upward, toward the clouds. "There's a *plane* up there somewhere, and we can't put up the antenna because of lightning?"

More strokes of lightning, two of them, really close, with thunder like the end of the world following immediately. Lex was nodding. "You got it. Too dangerous!"

Daley was out on the wing. "Forget the antenna," she yelled. "This whole *plane* is a lightning rod!"

He had heard someone, he was sure of it. For a long count of ten he stood absolutely still, everything focused on his hearing. He had to ignore the constant rush of wind, the thunder, the splash of rain. Not them, something else, something that came from a living throat. Not far away, but not close, either.

"I don't wanna die out here!"

Yes, there it was again. A voice.

Jackson pushed through the brush, head averted to avoid the backlash of twigs. He had a pretty good idea of the direction, but with all the uproar going on, he couldn't be sure how far away the person was.

Didn't sound like Abby, and it sure didn't

sound like Captain Russell. He didn't know Ian or Jory well—it might be one of them, might not.

It was dark, that was the trouble—pitch-dark, dark as midnight in the belly of a whale. The storm had brought on a deeper, sudden night. Yet somewhere far up above the trees, lightning danced, and light from nearby bolts penetrated the canopy of leaves overhead. They gave everything a momentary, green-tinged glow, just sufficient for him to get his bearings.

He heard someone whimpering, not far now. A convenient flicker of lightning gave him enough light to see a mostly fallen tree trunk just ahead, and sitting huddled under it a dark form. A boy, not Lex or Nathan.

Jackson sighed. Only one other choice.

Eric sat all balled up, his hands crossed over his head.

"Hey," Jackson yelled at him. "Better get out of there. You might get fried."

Eric exploded, leaping out from under the tree, rising to his feet so fast it looked like a magic trick. Presto Erico, and there he was, his eyes staring, his mouth hanging open. He charged forward, whooping, and to Jackson's amazement—and discomfort—Eric hugged him.

"Hey!" Jackson pushed away. He was wearing a rain poncho, but Eric was in a stupid little hooded sweat jacket. He was drenched, caked with mud, and maybe plastered with leeches. "Easy, man."

Eric hung onto him, babbling: "Yes! I'm saved! Hey, man, I've—I've been looking for you all over! We, you, it's—it's all right, you can come back, it's okay with everyone, we want you back in camp, and—and—"

Jackson waited for him to run down. He did after a few more seconds of incoherent stammering and jabbering.

Into the silence, Jackson dropped one word, like a stone falling into water: "Really?" His tone was skeptical, disbelieving.

"Uh—yeah."

"I'm not going back."

Eric moaned. "Oh, come on, man!"

"You can go back. Tell them you saw me and that I'm all right."

Eric was rubbing a palm over his face. "Tell them—right, okay. I'll just, uh, I'll go back to camp and tell . . . the others . . . only—"

"What?"

Thunder sounded again, like an enormous boulder trundling down the hill above them. With his voice rising to a panicky note, Eric asked, "Do you know which way camp is?"

Oh, man. Jackson couldn't believe this guy. He grabbed Eric's shoulders, spun him, and said, "That way, straight ahead of you. It's maybe a mile. Keep going straight, and stay away from tall trees."

He turned on his heel and walked away into the storm, leaving Eric alone.

SEVENTEEN

The five of them clustered beside the downed plane, making a loose circle. No one paid any attention to the torrent anymore. They were all as wet as they could get, anyway.

"This is stupid!" Taylor bawled in her spoiled-rich-girl voice, leaning on the wing. "Put the antenna up, Nathan!"

Nathan was just about fed up with Taylor's yelling. He was fed up with everything, in fact—of Lex bossing him around, of Daley's competitive self-assurance, of Melissa's wishy-washy efforts to get along with, well, *everyone*. With Jackson for deserting them. With Eric, too, for stirring up all this trouble. Most of all with Eric, who couldn't keep his big mouth—

"Go ahead, put it back up," Taylor yelled again,

pointing up at the roof of the plane as lightning flashed nearby.

Nathan snatched the antenna up from where he had dropped it and thrust it toward Taylor. "You want it up so bad, *you* put it up!"

"Don't be like that! I don't know *how*!" Taylor whimpered. "And anyway, my foot hurts!"

"This is torture," Melissa said in a voice that sounded ready to break into sobs. "What can we do?"

"We can get away from this plane, for starters," Daley said. "We shouldn't be anywhere near it. If lightning hits it, we could all get killed."

Lex chimed in. "Look, guys, it's a no-brainer. We need to wait until the storm passes over, and then we can get the antenna up really high—"

"No!" Taylor slapped the airplane wing, making a hollow gong sound. "We've got to call them right now, while they're close enough to hear! You guys said you heard someone trying to get through. Rescue is, like, right there!"

Oh, man, oh, man . . . Nathan wouldn't say it, but deep down, well, he agreed with Taylor. Of all people.

Another flare of lightning, another startling crack of thunder. Nathan made up his mind. "Daley, you're right. It's dangerous down here on the beach. You get everyone back up to the camp."

With an edge of suspicion in her voice, Daley

asked, "What? Why? What are you gonna do?"

Trying to make his tone casual and confident, Nathan assured her, "Nothing dangerous. Relax. I'm just going to unhook the radio and bring it up to the tents. Go on, now. We're like sitting ducks down here."

"But the radio—" Taylor began.

"I'll bring the radio!" Nathan shouted. "Daley, please, get everyone back to camp!"

Daley clapped her hands in front of her, as if she were shooing away an annoying puppy. "Okay, okay. You heard him, everyone! Let's get back to the tent and get dry if we can. Lean on me, Taylor—"

"I got her," Melissa said.

Nathan felt abandoned as they all started uphill. From the seething darkness, he heard Daley's soft, urgent voice: "Hurry."

And then he stood alone. Nathan stooped, picked up the antenna, which lay where Taylor had dropped it. Three lightning flashes, one right after the other, gave him a quick view of the plane. The wires that had led up to the antenna trailed out the open door. The wind had blown them back around to this side.

The thunder crashed down, so loud that it made him duck away. Was it his imagination, or was the storm growing worse?

Nathan clambered back onto the wing. In the darkness, he could just make out the radio inside the door.

He stood on the wing, clutching the antenna.

Man. He *hated* this part.

Nathan stretched up and reached out for the wires.

Jackson heard Eric behind him, screeching, "Wait! Wait!"

Jackson didn't slow as he heard Eric stumbling up behind him. If Eric wanted to tag along, just let him try. He could lose Eric in five minutes. Maybe then he would—

But Eric was right behind him, chattering, as annoying as a buzzing, biting fly. "Come on, chief," he insisted in a wheedling tone. "You've got to come back."

"Do I? Why?"

"You need us!"

Three quick snaps of lightning and an unearthly roar of thunder and Eric yelped in alarm. Jackson wondered what was keeping him from grabbing hold of his hand like a frightened toddler. "That's what you think," Jackson said as soon as he could make his voice heard again. "You're wrong, Eric. I *don't* need you." He took in a deep breath. "And you sure don't need me. You told me you didn't, remember? In fact, you were the spokesman."

He turned again, hoping this time Eric would just stay behind, would just leave him alone.

He hadn't asked for any of this, hadn't wanted the leadership, hadn't—

"Wait! Please."

Something desperate in Eric's voice stopped Jackson in his tracks. Eric had never sounded so forlorn, so much like—well, like a little kid. Jackson turned toward him again, unable to see him in the thick night but sensing him standing a few paces away.

Miserably, Eric confessed, "All right, I'm scared."

"It's about time you got scared!" Jackson snapped.

"H-huh?"

Jackson's frustration boiled over. "You haven't taken anything seriously since day one! What do you think this is, man, a *game*? Some kind of *adventure*? I'll tell you what it is: life or death!"

He bit back more words. From the beginning, Jackson had the heavy feeling hanging on him that their chances were slim, that they probably would never make it back alive. And none of the others had taken it seriously, none of them had been scared enough!

In the dark, he shook his head. No, that was too harsh. Daley and Nathan had tried their best, he conceded that. And Lex, sure, and Melissa worked hard—

But Jackson had been the one who was looking into the face of the threat and seeing death there.

Eric was still blubbering. "Well, I'm scared now! Does that satisfy you? I admit it! I'm lost, and I'm scared." He was sobbing now, like a remorseful little boy asking his dad for forgiveness. Please, please, I didn't really mean to break your calculator, Dad. I didn't mean to make an F on my algebra test. I didn't mean to back your car into a tree.

But Eric was saying, "I'm a jerk, all right? What can I say? I was wrong, man. I'm sorry I gave up your secret."

"Are you?"

"Yes!" The one word sounded as if Eric had wrenched it up from his guts. "Yes, I am!" He was actually crying now. "And—and I can't get back on my own, not in this storm. I really need your help, man."

Jackson took a deep breath. The rain had slacked, then poured again, and now was medium, somewhere in the middle, not a torrent but heavy. The lightning seemed more frequent, the thunder louder.

Behind him lay the hills rising to the mountains, the valleys between thick with jungle growth. He had walked a long way since leaving camp, had decided at last that he wasn't following the same track that Abby must have taken, and he had reversed direction to come back and attempt another path.

Captain Russell, Jory, Ian, Abby. They were

out there—maybe. If they hadn't drowned, if they hadn't fallen and broken their necks, if—

But someone was crying in the dark right *here*, right *now*.

Jackson grunted to himself.

He had to make up his mind.

"Oh, man."

Nathan fumbled in the dark with the bamboo pole that Lex had rigged as an antenna support. It had cracked at the base, but he had managed to wrench it loose. If he could reverse it, then maybe he could lash the antenna to it, not much lower than it had been to begin with. The cords were soaked, and he struggled with the knots.

Every flash of lightning—and they came in bunches now, more frequent, sometimes so close that they left a stinging odor in the air—made him cringe. He felt his fingernails break as he fought the wet cords. It was no use, he couldn't untie them. He needed something else, something that he could use to secure the bamboo to the snapped-short mast, and then the antenna to the bamboo. *Think, man, think.*

He was aching, chilled, and empty. What would his illustrious ancestor have done? Nathan could just imagine what he might have written:

"Finding that the emergency signaling device

we had was insufficient to our needs, I quickly improvised an efficient substitute using a handful of twigs, an ostrich egg, and a small snake, which served as the necessary wiring."

Come on, man, come on! Think! With a sudden burst of inspiration, Nathan unbuckled his belt and pulled it free. Maybe—

Yes! He wound the belt around and around, coiling it. The bamboo was up, the antenna was secured to the bamboo—pull the belt tight, buckle it—it was going to work! The wind shook and wrenched it, but the antenna stayed up!

Nathan grabbed the wires, twisted them around the two contacts. Did it matter which was which? Was there a positive and a negative or something? He didn't know. Didn't matter. Fifty-fifty chance of getting it right, better than his chances on some true-false tests he'd taken.

There! Now get off the exposed roof of the plane, swing down, climb inside—

In the thrumming fuselage, Nathan fumbled around, found the microphone, and picked it up. He held in the TALK button and spoke: "Mayday, Mayday. To, uh, anyone who's receiving this. We are the school group from Los Angeles that crashed two weeks ago. Call letters 29 DWN, that's Two-niner Delta William November. We have crashed and need help."

Nathan released the call button and listened. Nothing, no response at all. The radio was even quieter than it had been when its speakers were filled with static. Something was wrong.

Wait—the wind had yanked the antenna off, and then just now he had tugged on the wires. Maybe they had come loose.

He flailed around, found the wires, gently tugged on them.

They were disconnected on this end, not attached to the radio.

Great. Nathan tried to remember the setup. Weren't there two little knurled nuts in the back, and you hooked the wire around a post and then tightened the nut down to hold it in place?

Yes, here was one, and yes, the wire had already been crooked into a candy-cane hook. Operating completely by touch, ignoring the pain where he had ripped a nail down into the quick, Nathan loosened the nut, hooked the wire, and secured it. Now the other one . . . yes, that got it.

And instantly, even before the nut had tightened down on the wire, a voice flooded the plane, a man's urgent voice, clear and sharp: "This is two-twenty-four, Pan Asian charter. Please repeat, Two-niner. I couldn't read your last transmission. Did you say you were in need of assistance? Reply. Over."

Rescue.

Rescue.

The thought froze Nathan for an instant. Only for an instant. Then he was scrambling for the microphone, finding it, snatching it up, and stabbing down his thumb on the TALK button.

"Hello, hello! We need help! Flight Two-niner Delta William November is down. Mayday, Mayday!"

Nathan released the talk button.

The world exploded.

Daley suspected that Nathan was going to try something. As soon as the others had reached the camp, she had yelled, "I'm going back to help Nathan. You guys stay here."

Melissa yelled back: "The tent's gonna blow away! We have to do something, it's too exposed!"

"What?"

"We could drag it down there, into the low trees! The hill would give us a little shelter from the wind, and it would be safer—I think it would be all right, there's nothing tall enough to—"

"Do it!" Daley yelled.

"Come on, Lex," Melissa shouted. "Taylor, just stay out of our way."

The lightning gave Daley enough illumination to stumble down the slope toward the plane. Where was Nathan? She couldn't see him at all. Then she made him out, swinging down inside the plane. She couldn't be sure at this distance, but it looked as if he had put the stupid antenna back up, even after Lex's warning.

Daley fought the wind. It howled in, rising and rising. She actually had to lean forward to make progress.

The plane, at last. "Nathan! Come on!" she yelled, but the wind snatched the words from her mouth and flung them away.

She crawled onto the wing, climbed up, and then leaned inside. Nathan was on the radio, speaking urgently into the mike.

Daley had had it. She grabbed his arm and hauled—

A blast of lightning struck the antenna.

We're dead!

The world spun crazily. Something hit her back, hard, and she lay dazed, staring up at a fountain of sparks and a gush of steam pouring from the top of the plane.

Daley felt her muscles jerking uncontrollably. Oh, God, what had—

Nathan.

Nathan lay sprawled, facedown.

Dead! He was dead!

"Oh, no," Daley groaned, trying to catch her breath, trying to understand. The lightning had blown them right out of the plane, had stunned her—

Nathan coughed.

"Are you okay?" Daley shrieked, finally managing to sit up.

"What—what happened?" Nathan rose on hands and knees as if doing a push-up.

Daley shouted into Nathan's ear, "You're crazy!"

Nathan sounded dazed as he looked up at the smoldering plane: "I would've been cooked."

"Come on." She helped him scramble to his feet.

Nathan lurched and swayed, his legs like rubber. "Daley, I heard someone, maybe I got through just before—"

"Yeah, now can we get outta here?"

She was going to ache in the morning; she could tell that already. But Nathan was alive!

As they picked their way back toward camp, the wind shoved them from behind as if trying to get rid of them.

As if it had work to do.

The tent no longer tried to go sailing off into the night. The low rise of the hill cut off the worst of the wind. Melissa and Lex did their best, lashing the tent base to as many of the saplings as they could, until finally they couldn't take it any longer. Melissa had helped Taylor in, and then she crawled inside, followed by Lex.

Lex immediately found a battery-operated lantern and switched it on.

They all looked terrible. Taylor's hair lay in a bedraggled mass, and her makeup had run all over her face. Lex's hair had been plastered down by rain, and here and there twigs clung to it. His jacket hadn't been much protection. Water streamed not only off it, but out of it. His pumpkin-colored T-shirt underneath was dark with rain.

Melissa was almost grateful that she couldn't see how she looked. She *felt* like a drowned rat.

A nearby lightning bolt struck, making them all jerk in panic and squeezing another shriek out of Taylor. "Why doesn't it stop?" she moaned. "Why doesn't it just stop now?"

Melissa had no answer. She began to feel uneasy. How long had Daley been gone? Should someone go after her? She didn't know if she could work up the courage again. It had taken about all she had just to—

The tent flap opened and a terrified-looking Daley scrambled in, with Nathan right behind her. Both of them were plastered with wet sand.

"Oh, God," Daley moaned, collapsing. "I thought we were dead!"

Melissa opened a bin and began tossing dry towels to everyone. Daley took one with shaking hands and mopped her face.

Looking from her to the pale, shivering Nathan, Melissa asked, "What happened?"

Taylor wrapped her towel around her and clutched it, like an old lady holding a shawl. "Did you talk to someone?" she demanded.

Melissa saw Daley dart a quick look at Nathan. Nathan opened his mouth, but before he could replay, Daley interrupted him, her voice quavering: "N-No, we d-didn't get th-through." She swallowed hard and tried to make herself sound calmer, not quite so terrorized: "B-But Nathan almost got himself killed trying to save us."

Nathan's teeth were chattering. "I think I heard a plane. Pan-Asian charter or something. B-but then—lightning struck the antenna!" His eyes were round with shock.

"Oh, man," Lex groaned. "That probably fried all the circuits. I'll bet the radio's toast."

Nathan was trying to pull off his soggy workout jacket. "Here," Daley said. She peeled it off him, then gave him a towel. "That was totally stupid," she said to him.

He gave her a pleading look, and Melissa's heart melted. Didn't Daley understand anything?

And then Daley added in a softer voice, "And incredibly brave."

Draping the towel around his shoulders, Nathan gave a weak smile as he continued, "Uh, and, and th-then Daley came and saved my life."

From her place in the tent, Taylor made an impatient squeak. "Very exciting, you guys, but did you talk to the plane?"

"I *tried*," Nathan insisted. "But just as I did, the

lightning hit. Lex is probably right. The radio's probably useless now."

Melissa stared at Taylor, expecting some snotty remark from her. She bent forward, sniffling a little.

"Well?" Daley demanded. "Taylor, don't you have any criticism to make? This isn't going to inconvenience you?"

Taylor raised her head, and Melissa saw tears spilling from her eyes. In a broken voice, she said, "No. I'm just so glad you're safe. Both of you."

Melissa felt her jaw drop.

And at that moment, the tent flap opened and Eric dived in, a mess, dripping, smeared with mud, leaves plastered to his clothes and face. "*Whoo!*" he crowed. "Hey, it's a little damp outside!"

Melissa had risen to her knees. "Eric! What happened? Where have you been?"

"Give me one of those," Eric said, reaching for Lex's towel.

"Here." Daley flung one into his face, and Eric blotted with it.

His voice muffled by the towel, Eric said, "Everything's under control, people. When Nathan and Melissa turned back, I tracked Jackson down and brought him back."

"Where is he?" Melissa asked, bewildered.

Eric dropped the towel and spun around. "He was right behind me!"

Melissa grabbed a flashlight, stepped over

Eric, and pushed aside the tent flap. The night outside roared.

Jackson hunched his shoulders and trudged uphill. He would have to find some kind of shelter. He couldn't take his chances outside, not with the storm still rising, still pulsing. The worst hadn't come yet.

A beam of light, streaked with horizontal stripes of silver rain, swept past him, then came back. He turned and heard Melissa shouting over the wind: "Jackson! Hey, stop!"

He shook his head and turned away again, hitching his backpack into a more comfortable position.

Behind him he could hear Melissa scurrying up the hill. He sighed. She was going to take a fall, maybe break her leg—

He felt her hand close on his arm, and she tugged him to a stop. The flashlight beam found his face, making him squint. "What are you *thinking*?" Melissa yelled at him.

He was tired of being yelled at.

She pulled at his arm. "Come on—you can't go out in this—this monsoon!"

"It won't last," Jackson said stubbornly. "Let me go. I'm going to try and find the others."

"No! You can't do that!"

"Well, yeah I can," Jackson said flatly.

Melissa locked her grip. She was holding on like death itself. "Listen to me!"

"You'd better get back in the tent."

"I will not leave you!" Melissa insisted. "Listen! Whatever happened back home, it doesn't matter!"

Anger swept over him then, anger like a red, hot tide. He shook loose from her and stared at her, dim in the glow of her flashlight. "Yes, it does!" he shouted. Something tore loose inside, something he had tried to keep controlled, dark, secret. He felt it fill him, hot and bitter. His voice caught, but he yelled, "It does, whether I like it or not, don't you see? It follows me—it *always* follows me. You want to know what happened?"

His outburst had frightened her. She had stepped backward. He moved forward, bending, right in her face. The words came spilling out: "Okay, I'll tell you all about it. I went home! That's it. I just went home, to my old neighborhood! I wanted to tell them about this—this—" God, was he *crying*? He waved his arm, helplessly— "this amazing *adventure* I was going on, this trip to the South Seas. Yeah, I was bragging. I wanted them to know I was amounting to something, that I wasn't gonna wind up a—a bum on the street, that I was doing something worthwhile for a change!"

Melissa's voice came from the darkness, soft, but slapping him across the face like an open hand, stinging him: "What's wrong with that?"

What's wrong with that? Jackson struggled. How could he tell her, how could he make her understand? He was living it again right now, in memory—

"Oh, man," one of them had said, his voice a sneer. "You are just so cool."

Someone else spat.

"Come on," Jackson said. "This is the chance of a lifetime—"

The kid who had always been the one Jackson had most respected, their leader, shot a sharp laugh at him. "Listen to this guy! Man, you've changed!"

Jackson shook his head. "No, man. But this—I thought you'd be—"

The leader had boiled up from where he sat on a step, a silhouette in the dark, just as tall as Jackson. He surged up, shoved at Jackson, a hard jab in the chest. "So what are you sayin', man? You're, like, better than us, is that it? So we're gonna be street bums because we ain't goin' on your dumb trip, man?"

Jackson backed away. What was wrong with these guys? They were his friends—they were supposed to be his friends—

They were all on their feet now, all six of them,

crowding in. "I don't want to fight you," Jackson said.

"I'll bet you don't, man."

Derisive laughter. The alley was long, dark. The mouth of it was far away.

"Hey, that's enough."

Jackson felt a momentary surge of relief. Somebody had stepped to his side.

"I'll say when it's enough." The tall kid shoved the one beside Jackson. He cursed and swung. Jackson heard a fist hit a face.

And then the two of them were at it like a couple of fighting dogs. The others yelled encouragement, shoved the two together.

"Stop it!" Jackson was as strong as any of them. He waded into the middle of the fight, felt blows raining on his shoulders and arms, and shoved the two boys apart. "Stop!"

Something flashed in the gloom.

Something blade-shaped.

Jackson heard the guy who had stood up for him gasp.

"You cut him, man!" somebody shouted.

"Get outta here!"

Dark, running figures. Trash cans clashing to the alley floor. A woman at the mouth of the alley, shoved off her feet as the kids burst out.

Jackson had caught the injured boy. He lowered him to the ground. The guy was whimpering, "It hurts, man, it hurts so bad—"

At the alley mouth, a man had helped the woman to her feet. He was holding a cell phone clamped to his head, he was yelling, "We need the police, right now!"

Melissa asked, "So what happened?" As long as she kept Jackson talking, he wasn't walking away.

Jackson wiped his face with his hand. "I ran. I left him there, and I ran away. I heard the sirens coming."

Melissa's heart thudded. "Is—is the guy okay?"

"Yeah, an ambulance got there in time. Only now the cops are looking for me." His voice sounded drained, defeated.

Melissa touched his arm again. "But it wasn't your fault!"

He jerked away from her as if she had touched him with a live wire. "It doesn't matter! I was *there*!" He held up one finger. "I was where I wasn't supposed to be." He held up another finger. "Somebody got hurt." Three fingers. Then he jerked his thumb over his shoulder. "That's strike three!" He swallowed hard and looked as if he were forcing himself to control his emotions. But then, in a plaintive, lost voice, he asked, "Where am I supposed to go now?"

Melissa couldn't stand it. She lunged forward, threw her arms around Jackson, pulled him against her in a tight hug. She felt him shivering, sobbing. With her face pressed against his chest, she said, "You're already *there*. Without you, we'd be lost."

Jackson snorted and tried to pull away.

She held on. "No. No. It's true."

And then he was hugging her, too, holding on as if his life depended on her. He held her tightly, as tightly as she had ever been held in her life.

From the surging storm, Nathan's voice came: "It's true, Jackson."

Melissa pulled away at last. The beam of her flashlight was flickering, and the rain lashed harder than ever.

But they had all spilled out of the tent. Nathan took a step closer and said, "It's not just about you, it's about all of us."

Daley was at his shoulder: "We finally figured out how to make this work. Don't mess it up now."

And there was Lex, solemn as ever, but his voice sounded assured. "We elected you. You can't resign."

Eric was there, too, holding his hand out, as if a little uncertain whether it would be accepted—or slashed off. "I'm sorry, chief. I truly am."

Taylor hadn't come out of the tent, but she held the flap open. "Hel-lo! People! It's *raining* out here!"

Jackson reached out—and shook Eric's hand. Melissa tugged his free arm. "Come on. Let's get out of the storm."

He gave her a quick, tight smile and a nod. The others followed him into the tent.

EIGHTEEN

Dawn.

Sun rising clear from a tossing sea.

The whole eastern horizon a blaze of gold, under a layer of deep blue. Specks in the sky: seabirds, out for breakfast.

A wide trail, a ragged scatter of branches, floats in the water, spangles of green leaves spread far and wide, an immense feather-shaped plume on the face of the ocean, its narrow point toward the island.

A yellow plastic bottle floats bobbing by: SUNGLO, SPF 12.

A wheeling gull swoops low over the yellow speck, determines the bottle is not food, lifts again toward the glorious, wide sky.

The rising sun strikes its light against the rugged gray shoulders of an ancient volcano. The conical mountain rises quiet, no smoke, no steam rising from its crater.

But low on its steep flanks, a new scar has been torn in the dense green tropical growth: a bare gash fifteen to thirty feet wide, a hundred and forty feet long. During the night, an overpowering flash flood has ripped everything free, stripped away roots, branches, trunks, and soil. Trees, vines, underbrush, even small boulders, lie tangled in a house-size heap, blocking a ledge. Water streams from the mass still, trickling in runlets down into the jungle.

On the island's east side, tall breakers roll in from a still-troubled sea to thunder against the reef, tossing white sprays of foam ten, twenty feet into the air. The foam shatters into spindrift and mist, and in the level morning sunlight momentary rainbows form and dissolve, form and dissolve.

On the far western horizon, clouds, towering high, white in the sun but at their bases deeply gray, are moving steadily away. The storm walks on the water with jagged spider legs of lightning. The bolts are miles distant now, too far off for thunder to sound here, on the island.

Trees drip with a sound like a gentle spring drizzle. Insects tentatively tune up, then begin to chirr. Birds sing, take to the air. Below them, small living things creep from their hiding places.

They have survived a bad night.

The sun rises yet higher, looking down on the lagoon, the beach. The camp.

Scattered here and there ... traces. Things made by human hands.

In the stand of saplings, the girls' tent is whole, though its seaward side is thickly plastered over with wet green leaves. A twig like a talon, stripped bare, rises and falls with the morning breeze.

Its clutching branches gently scrape the canvas.

Scratch.

Scratch.

The tent flap opens ...

Nathan took an apprehensive look around. The campsite looked as if a hostile army had raged through and attacked it under cover of night. The boys' tent was simply gone—no, wait, there it was, far off in the distance, far off the ground, wrapped around a tree. Plastic bins lay scattered and spilled, their contents strewn as though a cranky giant's child had fingered them and flung them away. One bin, miraculously right side up, was full, overflowing with rainwater.

Articles of clothing and towels hung from high in the trees or lay on the ground, spread in a swath of destruction leading westward, away from the tent site. "Whoa," Nathan said, half to himself.

Eric came out behind him, stood blinking in the morning light. None of them had slept much, and he looked as drawn-out as Nathan felt.

But of course, he had a joke: "Man," he said, reeling around, his arms outflung. "That was some party!"

Lex had climbed to the top of the low hill that had given the tent enough protection from the gales for it to remain standing. He turned toward the ocean, shading his eyes, and then shouted, "Guys! Come here, quick!" He ran forward, vanishing over the crest, heading toward the beach.

Everyone ran after him, even Taylor, who determinedly limped along, putting as little weight as she could on her injured foot.

Nathan topped the rise and saw Lex standing at the tree line, staring down at the beach, at—

Then it hit him.

From somewhere close behind him, he heard Daley whisper, "Oh, man."

Nathan felt like collapsing.

The plane was . . .

Gone.

They all walked, stiff-legged, down onto the sand.

Part of the starboard wing remained, yards from where the plane had been, its root trailing wires and pipes. Other broken debris littered the sand.

The radio—
The emergency supplies—
The downed plane would have been visible to rescuers—

Jackson moved ahead of them all and found something else half-buried on the beach. It was sort of oval-shaped, flattened at the bottom. He picked it up, shaking from it a layer of caked wet sand.

Nathan recognized it as an interior door, maybe the one that had opened to the compartment where the life raft, the emergency supplies, had been stored. The storm must have ripped it free of its hinges. What use was it now? He felt numb.

Jackson banged the detached door down on its flat edge, shaking more sand off it.

Taylor brought up the rear. She stood staring helplessly at the beach, at the litter of metal and plastic that was all the storm had left of the plane. "Now what do we do?" she asked in a fearful voice.

Jackson took a few steps toward them. With a sudden, forceful motion, he jammed the door down into the wet sand. It crunched in, went deep enough so that when Jackson released it, it stood there, like a shield.

Or like a tombstone, Nathan thought.

But Jackson didn't look mournful. He looked defiant.

He said simply, "We start again."

They took a step closer together.

Nathan felt a hand on his arm. Daley.

Eric stood off to one side, supporting Taylor.

Lex was already scavenging through the wreckage on the beach, busy as a crab.

From the other side of Daley, a worried Melissa said, "Start again? But we'll have to start—"

Jackson's voice was hard, but not harsh:

"From scratch."

You know the seven castaways and you know how hard they've worked to survive. But did you ever wonder what life was like for Daley, Lex, Nathan, Taylor, Eric, Melissa, and Jackson before they crash-landed? Well, turn the page to find out in a sneak peek of *Flight 29 Down Prequel: Ten Rules*, and discover just how the gang battled a whole different type of disaster—high school . . .

ONE

Nathan

Hey, so my name is Nathan McHugh.

I attend The Hartwell School, outside Los Angeles. I'm recording this videotape for my short video project in Mrs. Ralph's media arts class. My video is called—ta da!—How To Get Elected President of the Senior Class.

Just in case you're wondering, yeah, I'm running for president of the class. I expect to win. No biggie. I've been president of our class for two years running.

Why do I get elected every time? Because I've figured out a strategy that works.

So here it is, guys: Ten simple rules for how to get elected president of your high school class.

What I'm going to do is videotape everything I do as I run for president this year, show how the ten rules I've developed play out in the real world. Then you can see how it's done.

Oh, no, I'm gonna be late to school! Gotta roll.

Nathan was in a huge rush. The deadline to sign up for the student council race was at the end of first period. His father had let him drive the Beemer for the first time and he had driven a little bit out of the way just to see what it was like to unwind the big V8 engine. Only . . . he'd gotten kind of turned around on the far side of Brentwood, and now he was not just late for school—he was in danger of missing the deadline to sign up for the class president race.

Class president! He'd been class president two years running—but this was the big year. Colleges really cared about your junior year. And if he was going to get into an Ivy, he needed every scrap of help he could get.

Nathan could see the Hartwell School as he came over the rise on La Cienaga. There it was— the beautiful rolling campus, with all the big oak trees and the broad grass lawns and the beautiful modern architecture. Every time he saw it, it made him feel good for some reason. He looked at the clock on the dash. Ten minutes till the sign-up deadline. He'd better hurry. He flew through the intersection. It was kind of deep into the yellow by the time he got through the light.

He was just a block from the school when he noticed the police car behind him, its blue lights flashing. He abruptly turned down the music on the stereo and pulled over, his heart pounding. *Oops!*

The door of the police car opened and a very tall, very muscular officer with skin the color of creosote climbed out. He walked up slowly, one hand on his gun, talking into the radio microphone on his shoulder. Finally he reached the window, bent down, and looked into the car.

"How you doing today, sir?" the officer said, with exaggerated politeness.

"Uh, fine, Officer, sir," Nathan said.

The officer had on wrap-around sunglasses and his eyes were hidden. "You know why I pulled you over?"

"Um . . ." Nathan swallowed. "I'm not sure."

The officer kept peering around the car like he was looking for something. He was chewing gum. "Nice car, sir."

"Thanks. It's my dad's."

"Mm-hm." The officer didn't exactly have his hand on his gun. But it was close. "You got a license?"

"Yes, sir." He started to reach for his wallet.

"Do me a favor, sir, just keep your hands on the wheel."

"Yes, sir."

"So this car doesn't belong to you?"

Nathan shook his head. "I go to the Hartwell School. I was just driving to school."

"The Hartwell School." The officer looked skeptically at Nathan, then looked over at the school. A lot of people assumed that because it was this famous private school, the students wore uniforms. But it was actually pretty laid back.

"Thought them kids wore blue coats and stuff."

"No, sir. It's got a kinda mellow dress code."

"Mm-hm." The officer stood up, said some more things into his microphone, then leaned back down. "License and registration."

"Look, sir, I'm gonna be late to school if—"

The officer showed a bunch of very white teeth. "You could have some problems other than being late to school if you don't follow my instructions very carefully."

"Yes, sir. Can I take out my wallet?"

"Slowly, yes."

"And the registration is in the glove box." He reached over, pulled out the registration, then handed them both to the officer.

The officer looked at the license and registration for a very long time, then spoke into the microphone some more. Then the officer leaned over and said, "Nelson McHugh, that's your father?"

"Yes, sir." Nathan kept looking at the clock. Six minutes. He still had to park the car and put his tie on. You weren't allowed to enter the front door of the Hartwell School without a tie.

A change came over the officer's face. "*The*

Nelson McHugh? You're his son?"

"Yes, sir."

"*The* District Attorney of Los Angeles County?"

"Yes, sir." Nathan's dad was in the newspapers pretty much every other day. People were always talking about how he might run for mayor or governor one of these days.

Suddenly the officer smiled. "Well, son, you shaved off a little bit of red light back there. But since your dad has done so much for the community . . ."

The officer kept leaning in the window. Nathan looked at the clock again. Five minutes till the deadline to sign up for president of the class. "Mm!" the officer said, looking around the car. "What's this got in it? The five point two liter?"

"I'm not sure. It's a V8, I guess." Nathan cleared his throat. "Um, sir? I really am kinda late for school."

"I bet this sucker must really move," the officer said wistfully.

"Sir? Um . . ."

The officer clapped him on the shoulder. "Sure, sure. Go ahead, young man. You drive safe now."

Nathan started to put the car in gear.

"Wait." Nathan's heart skipped a beat. But the officer was just reaching toward him with a business card with the LAPD logo on it. "Here you go, son. That's got my cell number on it. You ever need anything, you just call me."

Nathan put his signal on, merged slowly back into traffic, then floored it into the parking lot of the Hartwell School. If he missed the deadline he was going to—

Three minutes later he was inside the building, racing down the hallway. He could see the piece of paper on the bulletin board in the hallway outside Dr. Shook's office. Somebody was standing in front of it—a girl with long, wavy hair.

He slowed to a halt, nearly out of breath. "Hi, Daley," he said. "What're you doing?"

"Signing up for the election," Daley Marin said. She was looking up and down the bulletin board. There were a bunch of pieces of paper, each one with a different office on it.

"Where's president?" she said.

"President?" Nathan said. "I thought you'd be running for secretary-treasurer."

"God, no!" Daley said. "Are you kidding me? Harvard won't even give you a second look unless you're president of the class."

"Well . . . last year you were . . ."

"Oh, there it is," she said. She took out a pen and started to write her name on the sign-up sheet. The pen didn't work.

"Maybe you ought to sign up for a different office," Nathan said. "You know, I'm running for president, too."

"Oh, no, you should run for *vice*-president," she said, shaking the pen.

"Hey, I'm applying to Harvard, too," he said.

"Plus . . . I mean, it won't do you any good if you lose."

She looked at him sharply. "Lose? To *you*?"

Nathan shrugged. "Well, *yeah*. I mean, I have been president of the class for the last three years."

"That's because I was secretary-treasurer of the student body last year," she said. The way she said it, it was like she wasn't the least bit concerned about running against him.

Behind them someone cleared her throat. It was Mrs. Windsor, the school secretary. "Ten o'clock," she said. "Deadline's up."

"We're just signing up," Daley said. "My pen's not working."

"Actually," Mrs. Windsor said. "It's one minute past. You're too late. Sorry."

Daley and Nathan stared at her. She looked at them unsympathetically.

"But—but," Daley sputtered. "I've *got* to be president if I'm going to get into Harvard."

"Oh, well. I guess it's going to be Chico State, then," Mrs. Windsor snatched the sign-up sheet off the wall.

"This is totally unfair!" Nathan said.

Mrs. Windsor looked at Nathan, then at Daley, then at Nathan. Then she started to laugh. "Got you!" she said. She handed Daley the sign-up sheet and a pen. "Hurry up, though." She turned to Nathan. "What about you, Nathan? What are you running for, hon?"

"Same thing. President."

Mrs. Windsor looked back and forth between the two. "Well, now!" she said. "So it's a showdown."

Daley handed the sign-up sheet to Nathan. He signed his name, then handed it back to Mrs. Windsor. She collected the rest of the sign-up sheets, then disappeared.

"Don't come crying to me when you get rejected by Harvard," Nathan said.

"Nothing personal," Daley said. "But I'm gonna bury you."

Nathan laughed. Daley Marin. Like she had a chance of beating him.

"You really ought to go for secretary-treasurer," Nathan said. "I mean, seriously, you're not exactly president material."

"Me?" Daley said scornfully. She shook her head like she was feeling sorry for him. "I was about to say the same thing about you. You've been president of the class for, what, two years? And what have you accomplished? Nothing. You're totally disorganized."

"You're not a people person, Daley. This is not your thing."

"You always take the easy road."

"You're not a natural leader."

"You're unfocused!"

"You're uptight!"

Daley and Nathan's faces had gotten closer and closer, and their voices had gotten louder and louder.

There was a brief pause and then they both spoke.

"You're toast!" Daley said.

"Dead meat!" Nathan said.

"Settle down! Settle down!" Dr. Shook held up his hands, trying to quiet everybody. "Everybody sit down. I've got some good news and some bad news."

The camping club met after school in the Arts Center, a brand new building in the rear of the Hartwell School property. Eric McGorrill slouched in his chair and looked around as the room filled. Taylor Hagan came in and he sat up straighter in his chair, stuck out his chest a little, leaned his head back slightly. Then Taylor's boyfriend, Nathan McHugh, came in. Eric scowled. He'd been hot for Taylor all year. But how did you compete with a guy like Nathan McHugh? Mr. Nice Guy. Mr. Football. Mr. Cute Dimples. All the girls at Hartwell got all googly-eyed every time he walked by.

They had the big eco-camping trip to Palau coming up in two weeks. The only reason Eric was in the camping club was so he could be near Taylor. But the trip to Palau was going to totally rock. Palau was this little island paradise in the Pacific. The students were going to fly there and hang out for ten days. Most of the kids were talking about how cool it was going to be to see monkeys and parrots and all this dumb crap. Eric just wanted to see Taylor in a bathing suit. After that, everything was gravy.

"Settle down!" Dr. Shook said again. "Scholars, I've got some good news and some bad news . . . first, the good news. The good news is that we have an additional student joining us for the trip."

Dr. Shook gestured at a new kid sitting up near the front of the class. He was wearing a blue Hartwell jacket that didn't fit all that great. Weird. It was nearly impossible to get into Hartwell. And in the middle of the year? Eric wondered who had pulled the strings to get this guy in.

"Most of you know Cody Jackson. He just joined us recently. He's a scholarship student who is here on a special program called Operation Second Chance, sponsored by the mayor of Los Angeles. Cody, could you stand up?"

The new guy got halfway out of his seat, looking like he was bored by the whole business. "Actually, it's Jackson," he said. "Anybody calls me Cody, I'll bust 'em up."

The room was silent.

"Hey," the new kid said. "Joke." But he didn't really look like he was joking. *Note to self,* Eric thought. *Don't get in this dude's way.*

Dr. Shook gave a sour smile, then said, "And now the bad news. Due to the fact that Cody—excuse me, *Jackson*—will be joining the trip, and because of recent increases in gas prices, I'm told that the charter plane we're taking from Guam to Palau is going to be significantly more expensive than anticipated. The result is that the club has a budget shortfall of $2,300."

"What does that mean?" Daley said.

"It means that if you can't raise two thousand, three hundred dollars by next Friday, there will be no eco-camping trip to Palau."

There was a long, dead silence.

"But . . . we've worked all year raising money!" Nathan said.

"This isn't fair!" Jory Twist said.

"I know, I know," Dr. Shook said. "But I have every confidence that a group of young people as creative and talented as you will come up with a way."

Taylor raised her hand. "Why don't Jackson's parents just pay for him to go?"

Dr. Shook looked uncomfortable. "Uh . . . well, no, that's actually not an option."

"Why not?" Taylor said.

"I'm sorry," Dr. Shook said. "It's just not. End of discussion. You're going to have to raise the funds as a group."

Great, Eric thought. *More freaking bake sales and car washes. More selling candles door-to-door.* Not that he'd actually *done* any of that himself. But still . . . it made him tired just thinking about it.

Nathan raised his hand. "The car wash we did back in the fall was pretty successful."

"Not twenty-three hundred dollars worth of successful," Daley said sharply.

"I think we picked the wrong location," Nathan said.

"You mean *you* picked the wrong location," Daley said.

"Whatever. The point is, if we do it over in Brentwood where I live, everybody drives high end cars and they'll pay a mint to—"

"What about selling vegetarian sandwiches?" Abby Fujimoto said.

"Can I just say that's the most terrible idea I've ever heard in my life, Abby?" Eric said.

Abby looked at him like, *What?*

Kids started throwing out ideas for fund-raisers, each one dumber than the last. Eric stared at the ceiling. The car wash idea was about as good as it got. At least he might see Taylor in a swimsuit that way. Maybe she'd get all wet and—

"Something to add, Eric?" Dr. Shook said. "You're looking distinctly inspired back there."

"Me? Oh, no, huh-uh!" he said hurriedly.

A few more students chimed in. But finally everybody ran out of ideas.

"Anybody else?" Dr. Shook said. "Anybody?"

There was a brief silence.

"What about a contest?" Daley said.

"What kind of contest?" Dr. Shook said.

"Well, my stepmother's on the board of directors of the LA Zoo, and they just got this really cute, really rare monkey called a Palauan macaque. They haven't named it yet. What if we had a contest to name the monkey? It's perfect! A monkey from Palau. You buy a ticket and that gives you one chance. Then we'd have a big event at the end where there's a drawing, and whoever wins gets to name the monkey. Then we'd split the profits with the zoo. Everybody wins."

Eric rolled his eyes. Name the *monkey*? Trust a girl to come up with some kind of moronic idea like that. On the other hand, it wouldn't involve his doing any work. Definite plus. "Can I just say that's a really great idea?" Eric said. "I mean, totally inspired."

"Thank you, Eric," Daley said.

"How much would we charge per ticket?" Nathan said.

"Five bucks, maybe? If just twenty percent of the kids at the school bought a ticket, that'd be a few thousand dollars. And some people might buy a bunch. At the end we'd have a big drawing and we could bring the monkey and . . ."

"That's *fun*," Dr. Shook said. "That is a really *fun* idea!"

Daley walked over to the computer and pulled up a picture of the monkey off the zoo's website. It had huge brown eyes and spiky fur that shot up off the top of its head in a comical way.

All the girls ran over and crowded around the screen. "It's so cute!" they were all saying. "It's so *cuuuuute*!"

The boys all looked at each other and shrugged.

"You know what?" Eric said. "If it means I don't have to sit around selling cookies in the parking lot of some strip mall, I'm totally for it."

"What kind of doofus would pay five bucks to name a monkey?" Nathan said.

"I would!" Melissa Wu said.

"I would, too!" Abby said. "Oh, he's so sweet. Look at those eyes!"

"Nathan," Daley said, "you may recall that the last car wash we did raised about three hundred dollars."

"Four hundred and twenty," Nathan said. "Actually."

"Oh, terrific," Daley said. "That's only nineteen hundred dollars less than we need."

"Yeah, but I have the perfect location now."

"That's what you said last time, Nathan."

Dr. Shook held up his hands. "Okay, okay, guys. Tell you what. This name-the-monkey thing sounds great. But it's also rather ambitious. And we're very short on time. Daley, if you think you can put together such an event within the next two days, then go for it. If that doesn't work out, we'll have Nathan's car wash as a fallback plan. Deal?"

Daley and Nathan eyed each other for a minute, then nodded curtly. *What is eating them?* Eric wondered.